Bound
for
Hell

The Beginning of the End

French Royalty

authorHOUSE®

AuthorHouse™
1663 Liberty Drive
Bloomington, IN 47403
www.authorhouse.com
Phone: 1 (800) 839-8640

Published by AuthorHouse 10/26/2017

ISBN: 978-1-5462-1451-9 (sc)
ISBN: 978-1-5462-1449-6 (hc)
ISBN: 978-1-5462-1450-2 (e)

Library of Congress Control Number: 2017916424

Print information available on the last page.

Any people depicted in stock imagery provided by Thinkstock are models, and such images are being used for illustrative purposes only. Certain stock imagery © Thinkstock.

This book is printed on acid-free paper.

Contents

My name is Anoku, and what your about to hear may be hard to believe. But in the year of 2007, one would say it was the year I died, and they would be right. But what they couldn't tell you is, this is the year in which i was born....

My name was Anoku, and this is my story...

Chapter 1

G rowing up I never knew my father, but my mother would sometimes say I was just like him, but thats all she would say. She never spoke of him. See'ing as how I was a bastard child, the kids from the religious schools in my area would always call me mothers Sin, earning me the name Sin as I grew older. I guess it was fitting given how my life turned out.

For a long time now, I made my living as an assassin. One of the best money could buy. In this business competition is fierce, every ferocious man or woman is fighting for the top spot. The better you are, the better the contracts. Contracts other will kill for. The best of us, helps shape the world as we know it, from the assassinations of political figures to be replaced, to heading revolution in foreign countries. And then there's the game. Contractors putting contracts on the competition for sport, rich men making bets on who will win. I wasn't one for this part of the business, but its the very thing that brought my life to an end. And where my story began.

Everything seemed usual, a simple job, and some extra spending cash for a long awaited vacation for the love of my life, but like most things in life, I should know nothings ever simple, especially in this business. That morning we awoke bags ready and packed, I watched as my love exited the shower, a sight to make blind men want to see. Her petite, athletic frame swayed side to side as she crossed the room. Her jet black hair draped down the small of her back as the yellow complexion of her skin glowed like the moon in the sun light. She dressed as I arranged for a car to pick us up and take us to LAX, where we will take a flight to J.F.K Airport in New York for a connecting flight. This was fine for me, i'd be able to cash out the contract then catch the later flight out.

The flight to New York lasted all of three hours. As the flight came to the end, I suggested we take in the sights for a few hours to kill time. "Maybe you could do some shopping while were there, never know the next time you'll be on 5th Ave. Besides, I have a few business prospects I can tie up while I'm in town." I said as she smiled at me with a smile like the sunrise. She jokingly replied; "you trying to get rid of me? I thought you were supposed to be on vacation? "You know business doesn't stop because I do. How else can I afford to treat you so good?" The stock exchange is very competitive, and if I don't keep up on the trends i'll fall behind." It gave me comfort that she was naive to my other life, she was the only one I could trust.

As we exited the plane she took my hand, looking me in the eyes and said, "You know I'd still love you even if you weren't a successful business man, or didn't work so hard. I don't want you to think that's why i'm with you. I don't need any of this." She smiled then held out her hand as she continued. "Now give me your credit card, i'm going shopping."

We held a cab at the airport's drop off and lodging area, then requested the driver to head down to 5th Ave. As we reached 5th Ave the cab slowed to a stop in the cluttered traffic of the New York streets. "This will be fine." She said, deciding to get out there. I said for her to return to the airport when she was done, where I will meet her then. "Better yet. Why don't you grab a room at a hotel nearby the airport, and I'll meet you there. We can repack the luggage, and I want to take a shower before we board our flight." I said as she replied seductively; "We could always catch the next flight if you want a little more time for me to take a shower with you." I smiled handing her my credit card. Then thought to myself; the sooner we get to Africa the better, as she took the card then kissed me. She exited the cab and closed the door while taking out her phone to snap a picture. "What are you doing?" I asked. "I just wanted some proof that a black man can get a cab in New York." She replied sharing a laugh as the cab pulled off.

In the cab ride over, I thought a lot about what she had said when we were exiting the plane. I wondered, if maybe it was time for me to give this life style up. Just maybe there was still time for me to repent and make amends with God.

The cab slowed as I reached my destination. The lapse in time had truly escaped me, being consumed by thoughts. I had to keep my head focused. An old construction site for a renovated apartment complex stood no more than a block away. The intel said; "I'm looking for a city planner, and an architect going over some last minute design changes" and thats where I will find them. I asked the cab driver to pull over a block ahead, stopping at a nearby store called "The Bodega", I paid my fare and exited the car. The cab driver had offered to wait for me, but I explained to the driver how that wouldn't be necessary, I expected my lunch to run long. I walked into the store as the cab drove off, watching from inside the store window until he was far out of sight.

After leaving the Bodega I made my way down the block to where the construction site was. As I entered the site I could hear someone talking, from somewhere in one of the upper units. Climbing the stairs as I drew closer to the voices, they suddenly became quiet. I reached down into an open tool box outside of the door retrieving a hammer, and a box cutter, then cut a sheet of plastic from it's roll, attaching it to my belt to form a suffocation bag. I waited outside the door for the voices to start up their conversation again, but the silence was becoming suspicious, so I decided to draw them out to me, by throwing the hammer through the window at the end of the hall way.

CRASH! The window had shattered loud enough for the neighborhood to hear, but still there was nothing. "Something isn't right." I thought to myself as I began descending the stairs. Getting out of there as quickly as possible was all I could think of as I reached the bottom of the stairs. ("Ahhh…Shit!") The blade of a 3inch knife hurling across the room lodged into my left shoulder, knocking me over as my back slammed into the steps of the stairs. Rolling to my right side I was barely able to dodge the chopping blow of a machete crashing into the step where I had just been. It was clear now, that I had been set up, this was never a job, this was the arena.

Rolling flat on my back I raised my legs, kicking my attacker off planting my feet in his upper torso as he raised his right arm for another attempt with the machete. I rose to my feet cradling my left arm as he stumbled back into a wall. I recognized this man as I got a clear look at his face. And the machete, and hunting knife in his hands confirmed it. The Butcher; lucky for me, the butcher wasn't big on guns, because if he had been I would already be as good as dead. Even still that hunting knife and machete wasn't going to make this easy.

The Butcher had earned his name by leaving his calling card on every contract. He left his victims either maimed or decapitated, and I wasn't looking to be the next head on his mantel. He was more of a serial killer than a professional in my opinion.

He slowly moved towards me, watching my movement, and sizing me up. I could have pulled the knife from my shoulder to try and even the fight, but I would risk bleeding out from damaged nerves or an artery to do so. I slowly took my footing, looking at the piece of 2x4 in my right peripheral vision. As he got closer I reached over for the 2x4 and we engaged. Left and right we went as I moved back and forward, as he swiftly swung his machete. The narrow hallway made it harder for him to maneuver as I countered with the 2x4. We quickly shuffled our feet as I blocked his swings and tried to kick him off balance. He began pushing me closer to the stairs, making my room to move smaller. "I have to make a move and fast." I thought just as the hallway began to widen. His body shifted as he attempted a wide powerful swing, bearly missing my throat. I struck the back of the machete with the 2x4, forcing the blade to get stuck in a wooden beam, following with a left front stomp kick to the side of his right knee, dislocating it. Lunging forward he grabbed me around the throat with his right hand, as I grabbed his wrist with my left, preparing to break his arm with the 2x4 as his hunting knife struck me in the right shoulder. "Urrr…!" Blocking the next blow meant for my neck, I caught his left arm following with a strike to his throat stunning him as I twisted his arm spinning to the outside from underneath, then drove my forearm into his elbow breaking his arm. Dropping the knife he was able to catch it with his other hand lodging it into my stomach. The lost of blood I was already experiencing was causing me to become light headed, this was it, all or nothing. Giving it everything I had left, I grabbed his head pushing my thumbs into his eye sockets dragging us to the floor. I jammed my thumbs deeper and deeper until his eyes became mush around my thumbs, then finished with a crushing blow to his throat.

Struggling for air, I dragged myself to my feet, there was no time to waste, I was in need of medical attention. I walked to the door reaching for the door knob as it suddenly opened, stunned to my surprise I see. "Mie Love! What are you doing here ?…" (POW!) A single gun shot sounded. My instinct said snipper, as I pulled her to the ground, covering her while kicking the door closed. (BOOM!) Another shot goes off, this time I know i'm hit. Seeing the blood on her shirt I panicked, was she hit? "Are you hurt?" I fell back losing consciousness from the blood loss. As she stands

Chapter 2

The sounds of screaming people awoken me, but everything had remained black. "Where am I? Why is it so hot?" The screams began to drive me insane as they became louder, and never relenting. Suddenly it became quiet, and a cold chill washed over me. I can feel the presence of something here, but I could see nothing, there was only the darkness.

A voice, loud, but distant spoke out to me; "Who's there? Where am I?" I screamed at the distant voice. The voice replied with an echo; "Who are you?" I paused in the silence, then he spoke again; "I am you, and you are me, if you'll have me." I yelled back in frustration; "What does that mean? What is this?" It became silent once more; "I don't want to play these games, if you're going to kill me lets just get it over with." I yelled then waited for a reply. Suddenly the voice returned as he said; "You're already dead."

Just then like the opening of a flood gate, I remembered everything. Images flashed through my mind of everything i've ever seen. The look in loves eye's, and the pain of betrayal. The darkness quickly became a roaring fire consuming everything in it's way, burning me with an unquenchable flame that seemed only to grow as the images continued to replay in my mind.

Suddenly the voice spoke again, and the shadowy figure of a man began to appear through the fire saying; "If you will have me, you can have your revenge." And in all my anger I replied; "Yes… Anything." The fires then subsided as the man began to speak to me of many things. Rouge demons roaming the Earth. From rich ones to poor ones, and politicians to soldiers, even religious figures. All apart of a mass one world government ruled by Lucifer, but just as he once rebelled history repeats itself and many of these demons seek power of their own. And I was to be his weapon, sending them all back to the pit. And everyone who had a hand in my betrayal was on my list.

I was informed on my first job and told it would take place where it all first started, New York. As I prepared to return top side I as cautioned on some last minute details. "You are not the same man you were. You can be killed, but not easily. As long as you survive your body will heal itself on its own in time, but if you should fail, then I will be here to welcome you home. Do you understand?" He asked. "I understand. Don't lose." I replied. "And one more thing. If you so chose to roam the Earth, and not do the job. Well lets just say beware of the Jin."

The Jin, the elite of Lucifers soldiers. Fallen angels, more powerful then a demon. Demons were men of a wicked mind state given power from Lucifer. But the Jin were once angels given power by God, but fell with Lucifer when he rebelled.

I awoke in the very same place I had fell. It's as if time had stood still. I felt as if I had been gone forever, and yet it seems not more than a few hours had passed. It was like a dream, but my blood stained shirt was all to real. I stood up and walked out of the vacant building where I was met by a waiting 68 charger. Smoke gray with black racing strips, and a note on the window, with a picture of a man, and a address. I entered the car finding the key's already in the ignition, and a change of clothes with a 40 caliber Glock handgun on the back seat. I changed my cloths then hit the road, as the tires screamed and the super charged engine roared. It was off to the street races, my first target was a driver.

The car slowed as I approached a crowd of people with cars lined along side a vacant road that connected to the main highway heading west. I could make uses of the convenience, the sooner I finish this job the faster I can get back to California and begin my search for Love.

I could only assumed all of the players were here as I made my way through the crowd. It seemed I caught the eyes of the local thugs, and cheerleaders looking be taken home by the winners. While all the spectators who love the races, but were to scared or broke to do so themselves stood around the drivers. I exit the car and walked through the crowd, as my eyes shifted through the people looking for my target. When my course was altered by a voice inquiring about my car. I turned to face some loud mouth punk trying to challenge me to a race. "I'm not here to race." I stated "Well take your piece of shit car over there, and sit your bitch ass on the sideline if you're scared." I figured if i kick his ass it should draw a crowd and I'll be able to find my man if he's here."

Just as I began to step in his face, a voice spoke up from the crowd behind the man. "Hold on now, we don't handle disputes like that out here, we handle it on the track." I looked pass the boy locking eyes with the target. As he continued speaking as he walked over. "I haven't seen you around here before. You some kind of cop." I smiled as I began to reach for my gun, then thought about how reckless I was being. To shoot him in front of all these people would have the police tracking me all the way across the country, so I made him a offer. "You know what, I'm a little tired of all the insults, and you seem to be someone of importance out here, so I propose we race, you and me 5 grand." He laughed causing everyone else to laugh then replied. "I don't race for anything under 15." Either he was a potential driver for the Daytona 500, or he was trying to get me to back out the race, and that wasn't an option. I looked at him with a smile then responded. "You make it to the end before me, and I'll hand you my keys and walk home." He looked over at the car, A classic car in it's condition, he could get 25 to 50 grand easy. He thought to himself as he paused for a moment as if to think about it, then he agreed. Smiling as if this was a sure thing, he turned and walked to his car.

I walked back to the car and began thinking. "For someone who knows what we know, you would think he would be living a more lavish life style then a street racer. But I guess you learn to love the simpler things in life. Besides he had to know someone would be coming for him, maybe he just didn't care. "No matter, we were all on borrowed time anyway, and now his was finally up". Just as I opened the car door I heard a cell phone ringing from inside. I hop'ed in closing the door behind me as the rings seemed to admit loudly from the glove box. I reached into the glove box and pulled out a phone. There was no number on the display, but the phone continued to ring. "Hello". I said answering the phone. The cold silence on the receiver was as if the phone had went dead. I started to hang up the phone when suddenly a voice crackled over a staticed line. "The young man you encountered is one of us". I immediately recognized the voice as it continued. "He is how you knew where to find him. Your next target has been selected, leave no witnesses. Our asset will help you clean up". I paused for a second then replied. "I don't have enough artillery to make that order, besides you only sent me to collect him, but I'll make it clean. Who is the next target, are they here ?" The phone had become silent once more. "Hello, Hello ..." I said, but there was no answer.

I took a deep breath as I watched my opponent pull his car up to the starting line. Suddenly I got an idea. I opened the phone and called the police, giving them our location to be dispatched to the highway patrol. Once I finished, I started the car then pulled up to the line beside him. Then signaled letting him know to roll down his window. As he did I said to him. "You were right, I am a cop. The highway patrol should be here to arrest everyone any minute now. But I'll tell you what, racer to racer. You can tell all these people to get a head start out of here, and if you beat me you deserve to go free." He paused in silence for moment as if to study the sincerity in my eyes, then suddenly he replied. "How do I know you want just arrest me even after I win ?" I could see it in his eyes, he had no intentions in being caught, nor was he planning to stop,win or lose once his car got going. "You don't. But you don't have a lot of time or another choice." He looked to his friend and ordered him to get everyone out of here as he began to rev his engine.

Everyone began to scatter as the man ran through the crowd screaming. "The cops are coming everyone out !" You can hear the sirens and see the lights in the distance. He looked over at me anxious with a nervous sweat, The stakes for him had never been higher, only if he knew how high they really were.

The charger roared like the sound of an angry beast, lifting off it's front two wheels like a stallion hurling forward on it's rear screaming tires. There was nothing left to be said. We were now barreling down the highway at speeds above 130 mph; . Half way through I was expecting him to let of the gas, and began barreling down in the other direction. Maybe he expected there to be more police waiting down that way, or maybe it was just the thrill of such a close race. Either way he wanted to win, he needed to win.

Both cars were neck and neck, each one inching forward for the lead as the other countered. As we neared the end of the line, I could see the sign that marked the finish, reading. "2 miles next exit." I let off the gas giving him the lead. I could have pushed it into over drive and really seen what the car could do, but I didn't. He leaped forward passing the sign before me, as he kept going barreling down the road at high speed. I shifted my head lights off to appear as the distance between us had become great, signaling that he was free.

Some ways down the road was a road side rest stop, where I decided to pull over. I know a car like his wouldn't be street legal, and with his friends long gone with the hauling trailer, he would need some where to lay low till he could arrange to be picked up. So it came as no surprise to me seeing his car parked behind a big rig.

Still inside relishing from his victory, I was able to park the car . and approach his vehicle without alarm. Undetected caused from a false sense of comfort, and security from a recently obtained victory. It's common for most people to let their guard down right after a victory in order to celebrate a triumphant win of high stakes. As he relaxed resting the back of his neck on the head rest, he stared into the ceiling, or perhaps resting with his eye's closed. I opened the passenger side door, and quickly took a seat next to him. "Don't move." I said, as he become startled by my sudden appearance. "I guess your going back on your deal." He said in frustration."So what ? I take it your going to arrest me now ?" He continued. "No. I owe you a car for winning right." I replied. He paused at my response as if he was wondering if this was a trick. "Are you serious ?" He asked with a half smile. "There it is right there." I said pointing over his shoulder out the driver window. He turned aroud looking out the window. "Where ?" He asked turning back to face me. Only to be staring down the suppressed barrel of a 40 cal. A single muffled flash, and the back of his head opened up from the pressure of the 40 cal at close range. His body jerked back into the driver door, and like that he was gone, and so was I. The dead silence of the night let my mind wonder as the roaring of the charger echo'ed through the empty road. For a demon I wondered. My first target seemed very nieve, but I guess we can't all be kings. I didn't feel the slightest ounce of fatigue, hunger, nor yarn for a wink of sleep as I drove. Just the over whelming lust to kill.

The sudden ringing of the phone snapped me out of my trans of thoughts. No number showed on the display. "Hello" I answered. "Well done." The voice replied. "I received a present on my door step. I was beginning to think it wasn't coming." He said as he continued. "Oh you of little faith." I responded. "And the job was clean. Im sure he found time to brag about his victory to his buddy's as he arranged to be picked up. So as far as they knew,he got away from me. By the time they find him, I was nowhere around. He'll be just another rest stop victim. I stated as I continued. When he suddenly replied sternly. "I am not one of your previous clients. I care not for the details or the casualties that come with your job, only that the job is done. Do not mistake me for one of your clients who can't do this themselves or your friend. You are a servant to your lord, do best to remember that." I paused before responding. In order to choose my words carefully. "Your next target is in Louisiana. Head down south and wait for instructions." He proceeded on to say. Just when I prepared to tell him I was heading for California the line went dead. I guess I'm heading south now.

Chapter 3

As I reached state lines I observed what appeared to be the front end of a state troopers car parked behind a sign that read welcome to Langley, Virginia. It was a good thing to, it was far pass time for me to refuel, and try to get some rest. Langley Falls was as good a place as any, The sign read rest station and diner next quarter mile. Either this trooper was thinking the same thing, or I just picked up a trail. I hope it isn't trouble he's looking for.

Pulling into the gas station, I surveyed the lay out as I pulled up to a pump. The station was right across from the diner sharing the same parking lot. I watched through the rear view mirror as the patrol car pulled in behind me. I thought maybe they were attempting to run my license plate until they made their way into a parking space in front of the diner. I exited the car watching out of my peripheral vision as two officers exited the car still looking in my direction as they walked inside. Once I entered the gas station a young woman working behind the counter as a cashier clerk greeted me with a warm smile and thanked me for choosing to shop with them. I replied with a light smile nodding my head as I made my way down the hygiene section . I stopped to grab a few tubs of toothpaste, a couple of tooth brushes, deodorant, and soap. I figured it might be best to pick up supplies now. I could grab a room, and clean up after I get some rest.

The store was suddenly becoming busy as two truckers had walked in. I could only assume they were in need of coffee, and to refuel as one of the men immediately made his way to the coffee dispenser while the other to what appeared to be the restroom. I continued to browse around until I heard the door open again. As the door buzzed a young man in his late teens walked in. You would think at 7:00 a.m in the morning he would still be in bed, yet here he was smiling at the young cashier. She obviously knew him,or at least she had seen him before by the way she began to blush. I started making my way to the register feeling as if I had already been here long enough. I patiently took a place in line behind the young gentleman, waiting all the while growing more impatient as he continued to carry on a conversation with the young clerk. He obviously had no regard for anyone else that may be waiting. While continuing to play hard to get. The woman insisted he would get her fired if he didn't allow her to do her job, but his persistence never wavered, as he so eloquently replied. "Man this motha fucka better wait". That urge to kill began to rise inside of me as imagined wrapping my hands around his throat. "Bling, Blong". The noise the door made alerting you that some one had just entered sounded off again. The bells hanging from a string that was tied to the door handle jingled as the door closed, bumping against one another. "Morning Sharon". The officer said to the cashier as he walked towards me. At this point everything seemed to had been moving in slow motion. I was sure he was here for me, as my heart slightly dropped. This was just too many encounters for one morning. The cashier waved her fingers to the officer in a gesture that replied Hi accompanied with a smile. "Do you know by chance whose car that is out there?" The officer asked. "Which one?" She answered. "The older model car there on pump 3". Without saying anything her head slowly turned until she was looking directly at me as if she didn't know what to say, and was looking to me for answers. The officer began to follow her gaze until he locked on to me. Before he could say anything I responded."That ones mine sir. Is there a problem?" "Well no sir." he replied. "I was only admiring what a fine automobile you have there. I see you're one for the classics, must have cost

in the business of hauling, and I heard your story in there. If you would like, I would like to offer you my services, and carry your car wherever you need. For a fee of course. So, Where you headed if you don't mind me asking." I smiled in a gesture of appreciation then replied. "Well, at the moment I'm headed to get something to eat. Then maybe a room for some R&R. And although I do appreciate your offer. I don't think I could afford to pay you for the distance I'll be traveling." I could sense the slight disappointment in him as he shook my hand, and wished me well. How funny life seems to me now. Not being able to trust anyone. Fatigue had begun to settle in, and I had already had enough excitement for one morning. To deal with anymore cops would just send me over the edge. So I decided to make my way down the road to a near by motel. Lets just hope they have room service.

When I finally made it up the road I took a good look at the motel. Pulling into the parking lot I decided to circle around to get the full lay out, incase I had to leave in a hurry. I could see the manager inside, watching the car as I came around from the office window, and by the looks of things room service wasn't an option. After going around the complex, I came to a stop in front of the office. As I exited the car I noticed a pay phone outside of the office along the side of the front door. "jingling, jingling." More bells hanging from the door signaling someone had come in. "How may I help you today sir?" The older man standing behind the counter asked. "I'd like to rent a room for a few hours." I replied walking up to the counter. "Well we rent by the day, and its 50 dollars a night." He said while steering the contents in the white Styrofoam cup he held in his hand. "That will be fine." I said taking the money from my pocket. He began typing on his computer, then prepared some papers for me to sign, before handing me a key bearing the number 131 on its handle. I thanked him as I turned to walk out, when I noticed the small buffet of pastries, cereal, and fruit that he had set out. "Do you mind?" I asked pointing to the food as I looked over my shoulder awaiting his response, "No, go right ahead. Its for paying customers after all." I thanked him again as I began to take a little of everything. The vending machine in the corner was filled with various fruit juices, and sodas. I bought a couple of orange juices, and a bottled water then walked back out to the car. Once I was inside the car, I couldn't help but look at the payphone against the wall. I started the car, and began to back out when suddenly I stomped on the break, throwing the car back in park as I decided to make a call. "Dooo, Dooo…" The phone just continued to ring. I figured it was a long shot to begin with. If she truly was as good as she said, then by now she'd probably already changed identities. I had hoped she wouldn't feel the need, considering I was the only one who knew, and she believed I was dead. Just as I prepared to hang up the phone I could hear the voicemail come on, "You've reached Mie Love, please leave your message after the beep." A light shutter came over me as my heart quivered from the sound of her voice. I slammed the receiver down on the hook disconnecting the line, as people passing by cut their eye's at me. More people began to take to the streets as the day grew more awake. I walked back to the car trying not to draw anymore attention to myself.

While driving around the room, I found solace in thinking of how that phone line was still operable, at the less, now I had a lead to start from. It was a good thing I called from the payphone, just in case she decided to call back.

Once I finally was in the room, I decided to take a warm shower. The water seemed to have never felt so good before today. My mind began to drift as the warm water ran down my skin. Reminding me of the warm feeling of blood running down my side as my body became cold. My hands began clinching into a fist as I turned the water off, and decided to just get some rest. It didn't take long for me to drift into sleep. My body seemed to be sinking into the bed as I laid back on it. I exhaled a long deep breath, and just like that, there was nothing, but black.

"Uuhhh! uhhh..! The sounds of tormented screams were all too familiar. The unquenchable flames surrounding me. "Uuhhh!"

I knew this place. I knew it all too well. "What is this? How..? How did I get back here?" I found myself bound by chains to an invisible wall of darkness. "Hey..! Hey..!" I screamed, and continued to scream hoping someone would respond to me, but there was nothing, only the screams of tortured souls crying. And of those that continued to pray. "Was I dead? Had it all just been a dream?" Knock, knock, knock…The echoing sound of knocking continued to drift through the distance of the shadows. Knock, knock, knock!… The knocking grew louder as it dragged closer and closer. Something was coming, and it was almost here. Knock! Knock! "Huuu…"" I awake startled out of my sleep by a loud knocking at the door. I grabbed my pants sliding them on as I peered out of the window at a man wearing a blue suit. He appeared to be middle aged, and physically in shape. "He could be a hit a man." I wondered, but why, and how would he know where I am? Whoever he is, he definitely wasn't leaving. I grabbed my gun, and went to the door. As soon as he prepared to knock again, I slightly opened the door with the ball of my foot pressed at the base to prevent it from flying open as I placed the barrel of the gun against the door at center mass. "May I help you?" I asked through the slit between the door way. "May I come in?" He replied. "Now why would I want to do that? I don't even know you." I responded as he stepped closer speaking through the opening between the door way. "I'm a mutual friend of a friend." He said. "I have no friends, so what friend could you be speaking of?" I asked in a irritated tone. "You know of who I speak. Lucifer." He whispered into the door. "How else would I be here, and know, who or where you are?" I loosened my restraint on the door allowing it to ease open as he walked into the room. "How did you know, where I was?" I asked curious to know. He smiled then simply replied, "You don't survive long in this game without friends. You will do yourself some good to remember that. Because you my friend, are now a part of the fold. You should learn how to use those resources." "And how would I do that?" He quickly replied reaching into his inner coat pocket. "By doing what you are told and a whole network can be opened to you, helping you get everything you want." "Careful." I said revealing the gun, "Easy." He replied pulling out a wallet. He opened the wallet then pulled out a business card, and handed it to me. "I'm simply here to introduce myself." He said as I took the card from his hand. "A friend like I said. If there is anything you need, please don't hesitate to call. I know I won't when I need to call on you." He continued as I reviewed the card that read: Central Intelligence Agency. He prepared to leave as he walked out of the room when he suddenly stopped and said, "I left you a travel kit in the car. Some cash, passports, and driver's license in various identities. Also a few changeable license plates. If there is anything else you feel you may need, let me know. Happy Hunting." He said, but before he could close the door, I replied, "Wait! My dreams, why do I still see hell when I close my eyes?" He looked at me, and laughed then answered. "What you are seeing is a reminder, that your one foot in, and one foot out. Bound to hell, and destined to return." And with that he closed the door, and he was gone.

"Director Langley." I said to myself tossing the card on the dresser as I was making my way to the restroom. "Hhhhh." I exhaled a deep breath as I stood there over the sink. Its as if I didn't really recognize myself, I thought looking into the mirror. The warm water I began to run over my face helped to sooth my mind. The images of Love placed me. In one moment I imagined the times when we made love, and in another. "Crash!" The mirror shattered as I ran my fist through it. The pieces of shard protruded from my knuckles as blood ran down my finger tips. I have to get control of my emotions. If not, they could be my down fall in this business.

I cleaned up the blood after bandaging my hand. Pulling out the glass, and glazing the wound with toilet paper, then rapping with a torn sheet. It was nothing professional, but it would have to do. I gathered my things, and ate the small breakfast before I headed out. It was time I got back on the road. The new identities were going to make travel a lot faster, I could just fly there. I pulled the car up in front of the office, leaving it running as I got out, and walked inside. "Checking out so soon? You were only here no longer than 5 hours." The manager said as I returned the room key. I handed him an extra $100, and explained to him that it should cover any damages, then I walked out. As I got back in the car the phone buzzed alerting me to an incoming text message that read: "Keep heading south, and contact me when you reach Miami…" Langley…

"Damn it!" I said slamming the phone close. I guess my flight plans were out, and it looks like I'll be making a detour. I threw the car into gear, and started to pull off when, "Ring, ring…Ring, ring…" The payphone along the wall outside of the office began to ring.

Chapter 4

As the night grows old, the highway takes a settle ease. What was once high traffic full of travelers seem to become a ghost town, an empty road to no where. The quiet calm of the sun fall signaled the day had to come to and end. I couldn't help, but think about the call on the payphone back at the motel. The slight hesitation delaying me a second to late to answer. Was I really ready to answer? What would I have said if it was really her on the other end of the line? I could only wonder now. I thought of an old saying about the man who hesitates in war. He who hesitates has lost. And right now I feel like I've just lost an opportunity. Hesitation could be the difference between life, and death, too soon, and you loose. Too late can seal your fate. As I reached Miami, the city streets seem to come alive. Watching the lights as they lit the sky. I took the exit off the highway onto the busy streets. The sounds of music blared from every direction as people filled the streets. "South Beach," I thought. It always reminded me of Las Vegas with all the lights, and people. I figured I would stop to get a room at a motel I once stayed at, before I try contacting Langley. Pulling into the parking lot I watched as young girls took the streets wearing their short skirts, and bikini tops. And what looked like hookers taking John's back to their rooms. Even at night the bare skin of ladies asses hung out enticing men from all over.

I made my way to the office which was just a window with a slot box for handing over the money and information. I knocked on the glass to gain the woman's attention. As she walked over, she took a seat on a red stool behind the counter then said to me, "What can I do for you?" I asked for a single bed room, and the cost of a overnight rate. She then slid a register form through the slot, putting her face to the intercom and informed me that it would be $100 a night. "Thats fine," I replied as I took the form from the tray, then began to fill out the form. I reached in my pocket pulling out one of the identities Langley had given me, and a $100 bill, when it occurred to me. "How was it that all these I.D.'s already have my picture on them when I had only just met Langley?" Maybe I'm looking too deep into this. Life itself is a strange thing to me now. Deals with the devil and C.I.A directors. None of it seems real anymore. Who would ever believe it? I guess with those two resources along anything is possible, especially a pair of I.D.'s.

I put the thought to the side, and handed the woman my information. She handed me a keycard, and my receipt with the room number on it. I glanced at the room number 17A, then placed the receipt in my left coat pocket and headed for the room. I took out the phone and sent a text to Langley. Letting him know I made it into town. A warm shower, and some rest didn't sound too bad right about now.

Next door to the room I observed a man, and a woman who were deeply engaged in their affection for each other, sharing public displays of lust, like no one else was there. I entered into the room, and headed for the restroom. Seeing the tub I decided on just taking a bath. I layered back as the water felt so relaxing on my body as if it was rejuvenating. Thinking about rejuvenating, reminded me of my hand as I unwrapped it in surprise, it had completely healed not even a scar was left. I smiled thinking of the possibilities as I layered my head back, and began to fall asleep.

The sounds of dripping water echoed in the distance of darkness. The cries of what sound like an infant child screamed with a loud horrifying sound that could wake the dead. The cracking of a whip and unbearable heat overwhelmed me. I tried to raise my arms only to be shackled down by chains. I struggled as the warm moisture of blood started to submerge me. My heart raced as I began to panic, drawing blood into my lungs as they heaved for another breath...

"Boom!" A loud thump on the wall jerked me out of my sleep. "Boom, Bump!" Two more thumps and a woman's screams came from the room next door. I got out of the tub, and put some clothes on, when I realized I had received a message from Langley. I opened the message which contained an address and the name of a contact. After reading the message I prepared my things as the couple continued to fight next door. Three hours had gone by while I was asleep in the tub, but I felt well rested just weary from the dream as my mind made the adjustments to reality. "Du-dump, du-dump, dump!"

Loud booming knocks at the door alarmed me. "Dump, dump!" I yanked the door open to be rushed by a naked woman trying to run into the room. I grabbed the woman by the throat and slung her pass me to the floor. "Please, I'm sorry. Please just help me." She cried through her bruised, and swollen eyes. I remembered the woman from before. A fairly attractive woman with beautiful eyes, and busty breasts, now almost unrecognizable. I noticed the bruises trailed up her curvish thighs as she continued to plead for my help, but this wasn't my problem. "I'm sorry Miss, but you have to go." I said trying to help her up as she continued to beg. By now I figured someone had already called the cops and I wanted no part in this, but to my surprise, people were just standing in their doorways watching as they would a show. The man finally appeared from his room in a drunken state bearing a broken bottle in his hand. The woman cried out for me not to let him kill her. "Where are you bitch! My dick need to be sucked and it won't fuck itself." He yelled out in a drunken slur.

I looked to the woman then grabbed my things. "Just stay here as long as you need and don't open the door." I said heading out of the room while she hysterically thanked me. I closed the door then waited to hear the bar lock click on as I sat down my bag then walked over to where the man stood in his doorway. "And what the fuck you want?" He said holding the broken bottle up to me. "Auuu…" He gulped as I grabbed the man's wrist that he held the bottle with slamming it against the door rail as I struck him in the throat with my other hand to stun him. while I reached into the hip of my waistband to draw my pistol. I then struck the butt of the gun against the bridge of his nose several times until I seen it was broken. He fell to the floor nearly unconscious but still holding the bottle. I took my left foot, and stepped on his hand crushing the glass bottle into it. Then took the gun, and bashed his other hand, breaking his knuckles. I walked out of the room to find that everyone had gone back into their units. So I grabbed my bag and walked out to the car and prepared to leave.

The city lights seemed to dance along with the night stars. The cool breeze brushed along my arm as it rested on the window pane and I felt nothing, not a care in the world. I followed the directions that were sent to me. Looking at the numbers on the sides of the buildings, as I searched up and down the block for the address. I pulled up in front of what appeared to be a night club. There were people lined up around the building, all hoping to get in. A man wearing a red vest waved his arms towards me trying to get my attention. I pressed on the break, and allowed him to walk over to me as I gripped the handle of the pistol tucking the barrel under my right leg. As he approached the driver side window. "Excuse me Sir, I can valet your parking from here. I was told to be on the lookout for a man fitting your description, driving this model of car and color. I was advised to tell you that your party is waiting inside. Are you not here to meet someone?" The man asked while fixing his jacket. I looked at the tag on his coat which read: "Charles, Valet Attendant," before putting the car in park. I kept the gun out of sight, tucking it under the seat as I sat up then exited the car. I felt kind of underdressed looking at all the people waiting in line. I tipped the valet and thanked him, then headed for the club's doors. The two behemoths standing at the door stopped me as I approached them. I stood at "6'3, so I suspected these two could easily be "6'7 to "6'9 and close to 300 lbs by the way they were towering over me. "Can I help you?" One of the men asked as he crossed his hands down in front of himself. "I'm being expected inside." I replied looking him in the eyes. "Name?" He asked. "Samuel," I answered. "I'm here to see Samuel." He reached over to the other man who handed him a clipboard then said, "No, your name please." I glanced over at his companion then back to him and answered, "Sin?" "Sin who?" He replied, "just sin." I told him. "How did you get a name like that?" he asked. "I never knew my father, thus making me my mother's sin." I answered. "Aren't we all, aren't we all," he replied. He then made a gesture for me to spread my arms out as he began patting me down in search for weapons. He paused as he came around the back then pulled the knife from its sheath on my rear waistband. "Go right in, I'll just hold on to this." He said stepping aside to create a clear path to the door. As soon as I walked in, the mood of the environment was live. There were people dancing on the floor and lights flickering everywhere. A gorgeous young waitress walked up to me carrying a round tray with drinks on it. "Right this way please, your party is waiting." She said leading the way through the crowd. She rolled her fingers in a gesture to come and follow as she sashayed when she walked. Her royal blue french tip nails shimmered in the lights from the prop diamonds glued to them. The thickness of her body could barely be contained by her loose fitting sundress. Her ass took the motion of water slushing left and right as I followed her back to a booth which contained two men surrounded by ladies passing around a bottle of expensive alcohol. "Mr. Sin. how are you I'm Samuel" The heavier set man said pulling himself out of the booth to his feet. "A pleasure to meet you friend. Why don't you follow me so we can speak somewhere more private." I followed the man as we crossed the room to a stairway blocked by a velvet rope and two guards. The sign on the wall read private show so I assumed we were going into the V.I.P section. The two gentlemen lifted the rope and we continued up the steps. Upstairs the whole second level had turned into a strip club. We continued on crossing the room until we reached a door that read private rooms. We walked through the door then headed down the hall. As we were walking down the hall I couldn't help but think. "For a private room, none of the rooms seemed to have doors." I walked pass each room glancing in at people performing sexual acts. When we reached the last room on the right I walked in, and to my surprise I was met by the eyes of what looked to be a sexy hispanic woman facing the door on all fours in the doggie style position wearing nothing but a gun holster around her waist with a 44 Magnum in it and a pair of cowgirl boots. The sweat glistened on her body as the man behind her held the handle of the Magnum in one hand, and her hair in the other, vigorously thrusting back and forward. "And I thought I was paranoid." The man looked me directly in the eyes with a look that was all too familiar to me. His eyes widened as the muscles in his right arm tightened. I took a deep breath while springing forward in an attempt to reach him before he draw the Revolver from its holster, but I was just too far. Everything slowed to a pace like slow motion as I watched the gun come unhinged from its holster and his arm slowly extending out towards me. I swung my left leg in an attempt to kick the gun loose. "Boom!" A shot fired off just as my foot connected with the side of the barrel, but not enough to deter the slug from piercing through my right shoulder. My back crashed onto the floor as the man Samuel rushed towards the gunman. The woman took off running and screaming as she past through the door, and ran down the hallway. I scrambled to get back on my feet as the two men wrestled over the gun. "Boom!" Another shot rang out zipping pass my head lodging in the door beam behind me. The gun pointed into the air as they struggled for control of it. "Boom! Boom!" Two more rounds went through the roof causing the in the back as he tackled me into the wall. He followed with a right elbow strike to the left side of my head which I was able to block. He countered by gripping my right shoulder where I had been hit. "Ahhhh...!" I yelled in pain. My arm was beginning to feel better, but had not yet healed. I struck back with a head bunt to the bridge of is nose, disorienting his vision then kneeing him in the groan. He went down then sprang back up lifting me off my feet, spinning around into a slam as I crashed onto the floor. Countering with a up kick to the top of his head as he crouched over me. He stumbled back as the door swung open, and tree men stood in the doorway ready to fire. I rolled over darting across the room as they began firing in my direction. Then dove over the desk, listening to the bullets whistling as they flew past. "Hold your fire!" A man yelled out as the shooting ceased. "There's no way out. Even if you managed to, the police are downstairs waiting. They should be up here soon. So you should just come out and at least die with dignity." I looked over at the window contemplating if I could make it, and even more can I survive the fall. I grabbed the stone paper weight off the floor,, then peered out over the desk. I inhaled, then exhaled a deep breath. "Here we go." I chucked the stone in their direction running in a full sprint to the window. "Boom' Boom' Boom! Ahhh...!" I went down stumbling from a shot to the leg. "Get up!" I chanted pushing myself to keep moving. "Crash!" I went out of the second story window crashing into the roof of a delivery truck. I mustered up the rest of my strength to drag myself off the truck. "Ahhh....!" My legs gave away as they hit the concrete of the alley way. The shattered glass cut my hands as I staggered to stand on my one good leg. I held my side as a shard of glass protruded from my ribs and dragged my leg trying to hobble down the alley. The head lights of a slow moving car shined on me as the car slowly rolled pass me, stopping at the rear door of the building. I paused as the door to the building opened. Then watched as the driver got out and held the car rear door open.. "I know this man." I thought as he bared the striking resemblance of the street racer from New

Chapter 5

Beep... Beep... _. "Doctor Frances please report to the E.R." My eye's were groggy, and vision bleary from the bright lights. The loud chatter over the intercom blared in my ear drums. I notice the handcuffs latched to my wrist, and the railing of the bed as I lifted my hand trying to get the attention of one of the nurses moving about. "I have to get out of here" I thought to myself. Any minute now one of the nurses will return, and once they alert the police officers standing outside the curtain near the entrance door that I'm awake. I'll be on a one way trip to the county jail infirmary pending my condition. My body was well healed, and I felt no weakness from my wounds, but i was still woozy from the morphine drip in my arm. "Uhh..." Using my right hand i pulled the I.V. from my left arm, and begin to use the needle as a lock pick on the handcuffs. It took some work jiggling the pick, but I eventually heard the click of the lock release. It was time to move i thought reaching over to unplug the heart rate machine so it doesn't start beeping once I take the monitors off. My feet were cold on the hospital floor, and my legs felt flimsy as I stood up. The cold breeze creeping up my back helped to make me more alert as the flaps on the back of the hospital gown came open. "Where the hell were my clothes?" I asked myself wondering how I was going to make it out of here without them. I peaked out from behind the curtain noticing how busy the E.R. was. I could see the two cops holding a conversation. I eased back behind the screen as one of the officers walked over to the nurses station. I could hear him as he inquired about the location of the cafeteria. I took another glance watching as his partner gave him the ok, and asked for a cup of coffee. "No problem." He said walking off down the hall. "Oh, check in on the prisoner, and make sure everything is secured." His partner nodded his head, and began heading my way. I jumped back on the bed, and placed the cuff loosely around my wrist as I seen the silhouette of the side arm on his right hip. I closed my eyes just as he pulled the curtain back. The sound of his boots drew closer on the left side of the bed. I could hear him fumbling with the heart rate machine, and I couldn't afford for him to call for any help. So I created a sudden twitch with my left hand drowning his attention back to my side. He reached in grabbing my wrist with his right hand checking the condition of my cuffs. The second he lifted my hand I sprang into action rolling my wrist to grab his, then lurched over striking his throat with my right hand stunning him, and preventing him from calling out for help as he gasp for air. I continued following with another thrust to his throat, this time latching on squeezing in order to cut off his air supply. He attempted to grab, and fight me off, but the shorten supply of air made him weak. As his legs slowly began to give out. Ten seconds was all it took, but a good thirty would lock it in. But that thirty seconds seemed like a lifetime. My grip began to loosen as his body drifted to the floor, slipping out of my finger tips. I quickly jumped out of the bed, and immediately begin exchanging cloths with him. The clothes weren't a perfect fit, but it would have to do for now. After putting on the clothes I laid the officer in the bed, then peered out of the curtain to see if his was partner anywhere in sight. Lowering my head I slowly walked out. It was to risky to try the door. So I would have to make my way further into the hospital, and I'd better do it fast before his partner comes back, and realize he's gone. It wouldn't be long before he checks my bed site.

The hospital was like a maze from this side, each hallway and sign leading to another one, but the parking lot wasn't getting any closer. The doctors, and nurses gave me strange looks as I passed them going through my shirt then reached for the walkie talkie above it on my left shoulder. "Dispatch this is 642 reaching the parking structure, securing area for lockdown." I said into the microphone walking out of the elevator in a hurry. The second I was out of sight I began stripping off the uniform shirt, and ditching the police equipment, but kept the gun, tucking it in my waist band. I moved through the parking lot looking for a get away vehicle, something with speed. By now the police would have road blocks set up checking people, and I.D's as they leave passing through the check points, and I cant afford to be stopped. "Shit!" The police had began to walk through searching the parking area. As I turned, and started to walk in the other direction. An ambulance tuned down the row I was on heading in my direction approaching from the rear. I continued walking as if it wasn't there until it pulled up right next to me. "Hey!" A voice yelled out as I spun around drawing the biretta from my waist line, and pointed at the driver face. "Wait!" The woman yelled out. "It's me, get in." She demanded. "What do you want?" I asked keeping the gun leveled at her face as I moved closer to the driver side door, looking around profusely checking if anyone was watching. I took my left hand, and opened the door moving to the side incase she tried anything. "Move over" I said climbing into the truck. "Your the woman from the elevator right?" I asked closing the door then switching the gun to my left hand keeping it out of her reach. I lowered the gun about waist high so no one would see it. "You don't remember me do you?" She asked moving the hair from her face. The woman form the motel, I thought realizing who she was. "What are you doing here?" I asked. "Right now I'm trying to help you, so put this on." She said handing me a EMT shirt, and cap. "I didn't recognize you at first, back there in the elevator. I was just here to get my injury's checked out, and noticed you after that call came in, and you walked out of the elevator" She continued as I put the shirt, and cap on. "Why are you helping me?" I asked. "Because you looked like you're in need of some help, and the least I can do is return the favor." She replied. "Listen, you don't want to get mixed up with me, and I don't have time to debate with you about this, so this is your last, an only chance to get out." I said putting the truck in drive. "Well we better get moving." She said buckling herself in. "So how do we get out of her?" I asked as we started to drive through the parking lot. She navigated as I drove leading me to the exit. "Alright, hit the siren, and slowly pick up speed as we exit." I followed her orders as we came to a exit. "It looks like they're setting up check points, where not going to be able o get out this way." I said. "Just trust me." She replied with her finger on the siren button. When suddenly a call came in over the C.B radio. "This is dispatch looking for any available responders to a heart attack victim." "Thats the signal." She said hitting the siren. "They should have gotten the call to by now. They wont stop an emergency vehicle responding to a call." She said picking up the radio. "This is Adam 19 responding to the dispatchers call." She told the operator. "Adam 19 this is dispatch we copy, whats your ETA?" "This is 19 ETA approximately 5 minutes." She replied. "Copy that 19 please check your GPS for shortest route update. Hospital is under quarantine please reroute patient to General." "Copy that dispatch." She placed the radio back on the back on the hook, and smiled as she sat back. And just like that we had a free pass out of the as I sped out of the drive way with the officers waving me through. "How did you do that?" I asked. "How did you know that call was coming in?" My sudden line of questioning startled her as it caught her off guard. "Because I made the call." She replied. "This is so exciting." She continued. "I know how this all may seem, but this isn't a game. You can get in serious trouble. I appreciate what you've done, but I think it's best if I let you out now." I told her as we drove down the street. "I figure your going to need to get out of town, and your going to need some help." She said. "You've done enough already." I told her. "Pull over here" She replied. I pulled over, and stopped the truck as she began to get out. "Come on" She said. "Where?" I asked in response. "Its only a matter of time before they'll be looking for this truck." "How do you know all of this?" I asked. "Because I work for the hospital, did exactly as you asked, but we seem to have a small problem now." "If there is a problem, then you didn't do exactly as I said," Lucifer replied. "My Lord everything had gone according to plan, the problem is..." Langley paused for a brief moment before finishing. "You see I've seem to have lost him. He was arrested out back of the establishment, and taken to the hospital where he later escaped. The local P.D confiscated all of his belongings, and I have no way of reaching him." Langley continued to say. "This is not a problem Langley." Lucifer replied. "This is why your in the position your in, Find him." "But Lord if I use the agencies resources to locate a civilian people will want to know why. That could draw some unwanted attention on me." Langley answered immediately regretting it. "Contact our people in the Miami branch of the F.B.I. Have them take over the investigation,and retrieve his belongings. Keep your line open, and use your resources to monitor his phone calls. If he cant reach you directly he may reach out that way. No one knows that number, but us, and him. So if anyone is calling, it would be him and Langley... don't ever question my judgement again." Lucifer said before the phone went dead.

Langley closed the phone placing it on his desk as he leaned back in his chair. He spun the chair around facing out of the window, contemplating his next move. He stood up grabbing the phone, and his security badge then headed out of his office. "Hold all calls until i return." He told his receptionist as he began walking down the hall. Langley felt the need to call on his best asset, his go to guy for off the book projects. Murphy... Murphy was a wet work asset, once a member of the most vicious mercenary team, Dark water. Langley had made it a point to mentor Murphy, their relationship was like that of a father, and son. Murphy being young, but talented never asked questions, and Langley made sure he was always taken care of. If he never bit off more than he could chew, he could always count on Langley to get him out of the fire.

The elevator door opened, and Langley walked out, Entering into a bullpen of cubicles. He walked down the center aisle to a office on the left corner at the end of the room. "Tommos." He said walking into the office. "Yes sir." Tommos replied looking up from his desk. "Do you have any new leads on that terrorist call? I need something to take with me for my meeting with the President." Langley asked. "Not at the moment Sir, but I'll check with our assets and send anything I find directly to you." "Good Man." Langley said leaving the office then made his way back to the elevator.

No one had known why he was there as they watched him leave. But everyone had seen him, and that was just what Murphy needed to know he was needed. Langley went back to his office, and did as Lucifer had told him. He picked up the phone, and called their contact in the F.B.I to his surprise he had already been informed by lucifer. This didn't make Langley any more comfortable.

"Ding!" Faith pulled on the lever to signal for the bus to stop. "Come on." She said leading the way off the bus. "My condo is just a few blocks over." I continued to look over my shoulder as I followed her through the streets. When at last we had came to a pink colored complex along the water way. We walked in as she greeted the door man who was sitting behind a desk in the center of the lobby. Never breaking stride we continued to the elevator. Once inside she pressed the button for the second floor as she exhaled her breath in a sigh of relief. "You should be alright here for the time being." She said as the doors opened, and we exited to the right. "It's just up ahead." We continued up the hall coming to a door that read 218, but for the life of me I couldn't understand why she would go to such lengths to help me, but I couldn't complain about her assistance. She opened the door, and walked in. "Come in", She said holding the door open as she stood in the door way. I walked in as she closed the door locking it behind me. I walked over to the window, and peered out at the view over looking the water. She had a nice place, very quiet. The limited amount of furniture suggested she didn't entertain much company. "You can have a seat, make yourself comfortable. Im just going to take a shower,

I'll be back in a minute." Faith said as she walked back to the living room, and turned on the t.v. As I sat there on the couch I scrolled through the channels looking for the local news until I found it. I needed to know what they had on me.

"Flight 413 is now boarding at gate A3." The voice over the intercom said as Murphy exited the plane. He walked through the terminal carrying a black carry on bag. Dressed in a grey tailor made suit. One would think he was your average traveling business man. He stood at approximately 6'1, and 205 lbs with the strong stature of an athlete. His fare skin, and long hair complemented his boyish charm. Deceiving to all whom didn't know him, at only 23 years of age, he was as lethal as they come.

Murphy walked out to the pick up, and drop off area to hale a cab. He took out his phone and made a call as the cab pulled up. The cab driver exited the car, walking around to retrieve Murphy's luggage. "I'll take this for you Sir. Welcome to Miami." The driver said loading the bag into the trunk of the cab. "Ring, Ring...," "Hello.." Langley said answering the phone. "I'm here. What are my destinations?" Murphy asked as he was entering the cab. "His last known location was a motel off of South Beach. He may have returned there. See if you can find out anything, and call me when you pick up his trail. Make sure to use the safe house for a place to stay. Any equipment you need should be there." "Confirmed." Murphy replied before closing the phone. "Ok,, where to?" The driver asked as he entered the car. "South Beach my friend. Take me to South Beach."

Chapter 6

Ring, Ring,Ring... "This is Love." She said answering the phone. "How are you my dear?" A voice replied over the static line. "You know he was there at the club tonight." She answered. "I won't ask again, how are you Love?" The man irritated. "I'm fine. He was just a little too close. If he wasn't so wounded who knows what he could have done." She stated in an uneasy tone. "Nothing!" The man replied elevating his voice in anger." This is why you have a driver, and a guardian with you. Do you doubt my ability to protect you?" "No my Lord, forgive me." She replied hysterically as her hand trembled, holding the phone." Do well to remember, you live at my mercy. It would be just as easy to leave him chasing a ghost. Do we have a clear understanding?" "Yes my Lord." "Do not begin to ware out your usefulness Love." He stated before the line went dead.

Love hung up the phone then rolled over on the bed, laying her head on the broad chest of a man. "You'll always protect me right Aknubious?' She asked cradling her body against his. "Always." He replied. "Even against him?" She asked as she rubbed her hand on his man hood. "Who?" He asked giving her a kiss. Love begin pulling on his lower lip with her teeth, then slowly start to kiss his neck up to his ear, then whispered. "Lucifer."

"Hi, may I help you?" The woman asked Murphy as he approached the window of the motel office. He smiled causing the woman to do the same. Then pulled out a wallet, flashing a falsified detective badge for the Miami P.D. "How are you today beautiful?" Murphy asked continuing to smile. "I was hoping you could assist me with a small matter, pertaining to a tenet you housed here about a night or so ago." The woman stood there confused, and dumbfounded. As Murphy pulled a document up on his phone. The information of the alias used here come up as he opened the file. "A Mr. Jonathan Frances. Does that ring a bell?" He asked leaning his shoulder against the glass staring into her eyes. She began to blush like a giggly little school girl chewing on her piece of gum. She smile looking down at the screen, and typed the name in. "Just let me take a look one minute." She stated smiling back at him. "Oh, here it is. It says he had a over night room which was paid in advance, but he never checked out." "I see. Did you happen to see him come in with anyone, or leave with anyone?" Murphy asked with a curious look on his face. "Noooo.... But I assumed he was coming back before the woman who was renting the room next to him returned his key. Now I thought that was strange." "Yes I agree, very strange." Murphy stated. "And you say she didn't come in with him?" "Well no. She actually came in with another gentlemen, until the ambulance was called to wheel him out of here. Some type of domestic dispute, if that helps you in any way." "Well yes it does. You've been very helpful, and I thank you for it. Now do you mind giving me the names of that couple by chance?" "Not a problem." She said pulling up the information. Then wrote it on a piece of paper before sliding it to him. He looked down at the photo copy of the two driver's license, and a hand written phone number with a heart, and name following. (<3 Lizzy). He smiled at it, and thought to himself for a minute. Then said, "Your a very attractive girl Lizzy, but nobody likes a snitch." Lizzy jaw dropped, and eyes widened. A look of shock frozen on her face like stone. Murphy then turned to walk away as he continued to say. "You should learn to keep your damn mouth shut, snitch ass Bitch!" Those were the last words she heard as she watched him walk into the distance.

Murphy knew what he had to do next. He would need to run down these leads, but to do so he would need his own wheels. He reached the cab that had been waiting for him at the corner. Opening the rear door he slid in behind the driver. "Alright, where to next." The driver asked excited to have such a long fare. "Uptown." Murphy said. "I'll let you know when we get there."

. . .

Faith walked out of the back room fully dressed, as if to be going somewhere. "You're leaving?" I asked feeling uncomfortable about the idea. "Don't worry, I'll be back soon. You can stay if you'd like, although I wish you would. Seeing as how I'm only going to grab a change of clothes, and some personal hygiene products for you." "You don't need to do that." I replied. "It's really no problem, I'm sure you'd like to clean up." "Listen I don't mean to sound unappreciative, but at the risk of." "Please... Just let me do this for you." She said cutting me off in mid sentence. "I never got to thank you for what you've done for me. I have the tendency to get mixed up with all the wrong guys, and for the first time in forever somebody actually helped me." I could see it in her eyes this meant a lot to her, and all I can think to say was. "I'm no hero Faith." "I never said you were Sin." She replied smiling as she walked out, closing the door behind her. . . .

"Just up ahead on your left." Murphy said pointing to a high rise condominium. "Here will be just fine." He stated as the driver pulled into the drive way of the plaza. The car slowed to a stop near the front entrance. "Ok buddy, just let me grab your bag." The driver stated putting the car in park, then opened the door preparing to get out. "That will be fine." Murphy said stopping him from exiting the car. "Just pop the trunk, I can take it from here. What do I owe you?" He asked looking up at the meter, then reaching into his back pocket pulling out a wallet. The meter had read $225.00 dollars. Murphy reached into the wallet retrieving two $100 dollar bills, and a $50 folding them in half as he handed it to him. "You keep the change." He said opening the door, and exited. "Thank you Sir, thank you." The driver said as Murphy closed the door. Murphy retrieved his luggage, then shut the trunk slapping it twice to signal the driver that he was clear to leave. Then walked into the building. He entered through the revolving door taking a glance around the lobby surveying the layout as he exited. The lobby was a real lounge filled with lounging sofa's, and waitresses walking to, and from the bar to the seating area carrying drinks. "May I take your bag Sir?" The door man offered. "That's alright." Murphy said declining as he began making his way through the lobby, heading in the direction of the elevators. He took notice of the two security guards sitting in their booth as he passed them, reaching the elevator vault. "Ding!" The doors opened as he pressed the button. He entered into the empty elevator which ran off a finger print analysis system. Murphy placed his hand on the scanner sending a conformation of identity to the security desk. Once security was able to match the conformation with the list of accessible people. The guards sent the elevator up to the condo. The doors had opened leading directly into the room, as Murphy exited walking in. He dropped his bag on the long black sectional sofa then walked over to the fish tank. Murphy pulled his left arm from his jacket then rolled up the sleeve of his shirt. He reached into the tank flicking a switch on the sand castle. When suddenly the bricks above the fire place released, and a shelf of guns came out. Murphy walked over to the shelf retrieving a nickel colored 357 snub nose magnum, and a matching suppressor. "Ring, Ring, Ring." "Go for Murphy." He said answering the phone. "Murphy it's Langley. Tell me you got something.'" Langley asked hoping for a update of good news. "Nothing yet, but I'm on the trail. I have a few leads I'm running down, I'm actually on my way out now." "Well if you're headed down to the hospital it's a dead end. He was found, and picked up by the paramedics, but he managed to escape police custody. They got the area locked down, the F.B.I is now lead over the investigation." "That's good to know. I was heading to the hospital, but not for him. Maybe you can save me some time. I need a trace an on a Charles Walkens, Miami resident, and any local family members. I'm heading over to his place now." "Well who is he? And what does he have to do with any of this?" "I don't know yet, but you'll know when I know something." "Confirmed, keep me updated." Langley replied then hung up the phone. Murphy placed the suppressor in his inner coat pocket then tucked the revolver in the rear of his waist band. Fixing his clothes he pulled his jacket back on then headed for the elevator. as he reached the elevator he stopped, grabbing a set of keys from a key rack that contained multiple sets for various vehicles. He pulled on one of the hooks,, and the gun shelf lowered back into the bricks of the fire place, and locked. Now he was ready to go.

The day was beginning to wind down as the sun light started to weaken. It was just after mid day, and the day was drawing near end, or maybe a storm was coming. Murphy walked out of the elevator entering the parking garage. He pressed the alarm button unlocking the doors of a black Audi A6, then as fast as he could get in, he was in the wind.

Murphy drove down Kings Blvd heading to the address on the photo copy of Charles Walkens drivers license. When he received a call from Langley. "Go for Murphy." He said answering the phone. The two talked for a brief moment as Langley explained the information Murphy had requested. Langley had informed him that Charles was a construction worker of 12 years. a family business run by him, and his brother. Charles had a criminal record for prior drug abuse convictions. He currently leases a room to a tent, a Mr. Armstrong whom has a Military background of 4 years in the U.S Marines, and a prior conviction for possession for sales. Murphy received the information, then asked Langley to stay by the phone. He would be calling with more information, and possibly need him to run another trace. "I have to go." Murphy said then hung up the phone as he pulled up I front of a two story home. Where he could see Charles sitting in what appeared to be his living room through the front window. Murphy checked the casings in the revolver before tucking it back in his waist band. He exited the car, and walked to the front door giving 3 hard,

"Well that's why I'm here. Let me just get my pen, and some forms for you to fill out." Murphy replied reaching into his inner coat pocket for the suppressor. "I may have forgotten the forms in my car. If you'll give me a moment, I'll return with them shortly." He said standing from the chair, drawing the .357 from his waist band as he turned his back to Charles. Murphy begin to connect the suppressor as he slowly walked to the door. "Oh, one more thing Mr. Walkens. Twooth..! Twooth..!" The muffled sound of the muzzle was like the sound of a person spitting sunflower seeds. Two flashes went off, lightning the room like a photo shoot. Murphy narrowed the gun at the door way of the kitchen, circling around as he slowed approached. "Clack! Clack! Clack! Clack! Clack! Twooth! Clack! Twooth! Clack! Twooth! Twooth! Clack! Twooth! Clack!" The exchange of gunfire ripped through the walls, one a suppressed .45 caliber Smith and Western. The other a suppressed .357 both tearing through the wall leaving holes the size of a .50 cent piece. Murphy darted to the side diving behind the couch. "I'm all out, you hear me? But if you want to kill me, you do it like a man, and come get me." Murphy was smart, but as all young men with extraordinary talent, he was eager for a challenge. Seeing as how he was also out of ammunition this was his only option. Murphy began to take off his jacket using it to undo the hot suppressor from the gun. Clutching it in one hand, he yelled for Armstrong to throw out his weapon. There was a slight hesitation for a moment, then suddenly a gun flew out the door way. Murphy peeked out around the couch then tossed his gun where Armstrong could see it. "Alright! Let's go!" He yelled as he stood up, and walked out into the open. Armstrong peeked out noticing that Murphy was serious then stepped back into the kitchen where Murphy could see him. "Come get it." He said raising his hands, bouncing back, and forward. Murphy smiled then lunged into a sprint towards Armstrong hurling the suppressor at his head. Armstrong ducked then returned to his standing position only to be met by Murphy's flying knee catching his collarbone barely missing his chin. Armstrong's body slammed into the island counter in the center of the room. Unable to recover Murphy followed with a right elbow strike to the left temple trying to finish him. Armstrong reached out grabbing a hold of Murphy, then countered with a head butt causing him to stager back then followed with a right front kick landing in Murphy's upper torso. Leaping forward with a reverse punch, Armstrong hand crashed into a wall as Murphy parred to the left, quickly countering with a strong right hook . Murphy then followed with a pair of jabs, left, right, then a grapple behind the neck dragging Armstrong into a knee strike cracking his lower right ribs. Armstrong latched on to Murphy's arm giving a forceful swing taking Murphy off his feet, slinging him into a wall. Murphy slid down the wall as Armstrong grabbed a knife from the kitchen counter. Pouncing on top of him to deliver the fatal blow, Murphy suddenly kicked up from his back catching his arm preventing the knife from striking. He pressed against his arm as Armstrong continued to press down with the knife. Taking his left hand Armstrong reached around grabbing Murphy's neck attempting to strangle him. Murphy could feel himself loosing strength as Armstrong partially closed his airway. Releasing his foot, allowed Armstrong's weight to drop with the knife. Murphy pushed his arm across as he fell, and locking his legs around his neck, placing him in a triangle lock. The knife stuck into the ground as Murphy secured his hold. The tighter the lock became the more Armstrong suffocated. As he started to lose consciousness he could feel his muscles failing him as the pressure on his arm was near breaking. "Snap!" "Ahhh!" Armstrong screamed out as his arm finally gave out snapping in two. Murphy seize the opportunity to tighten the hold around his neck seeing that Armstrong had just released what little air he had left. His eyes became blood shot red as he gasped for air until his body finally collapsed. Murphy watched the drool run from his mouth as the life drained from his eye's. Releasing the corpse Murphy returned to his feet, then walked over to the kitchen stove. After turning the gas on high, he unhooked the line letting the gas leak into the room. He hurried from the

Chapter 7

"In other news, two terrorist were killed in an attack on American citizens at a Miami night club. Witnesses say the two gunmen were heard chanting anti-semitism against the West, and praising Allah as the two killed several people creating a massacre before being shot down themselves. We go live from the White House press conference for words from our Secretary of defense..."

"My fellow Americans, today we have suffered a tragedy here on American soil. I, myself, and other cabinet members are deeply grieved for the loss of those innocent American lives, and the family's of those who suffered injury in this horrific attack. I have spoken with our President, and he has assured me that we are all in agreement, and on accord. This display of hatred against our great nation will not go unpunished. We are narrowing down our suspects, and any involvement from allied help. This is and act of war, and we will strike back with such force as necessary to show the world that this type of hatred or any hatred will not be tolerated. God bless you all, and God bless America. Thank you..."

"Well there you have it, that was our Secretary of Defense we just heard there speaking live from the White House. Theres still no word yet to the actual identity of one of the victims, but its been said he's the son of a foreign national. If that is confirmed this could spark another 10 years of unrest in an already long, and gruesome battle for power in these countries. Would this spell new leadership, and how would this effect the U.S., and it's involvement. Stay with us as we continue this..."

I had heard enough. I turned off the t.v, and began to stare out the window for awhile. Becoming lost in my thoughts as my eyes seemed to stare out the window for miles. (Becoming lost in my thoughts as my eyes seemed to stare a thousand yards off.) This wasn't anything I hadn't been apart of before. One man dies, and 10 thousand more followed, but what was different now? I guess knowing what's behind the curtain changes things. So many innocent people, children naive to it all, but die all the same in war. "Was he really some type of prince, or just another demon? Why else would they send me there?" . . .

"Love! It's time to go." Aknubious yelled as he stood at the door with luggage in hand. "Im coming, it is a private jet. It's not like we're going to be late." She replied pulling on her heels as she walked down the hallway. "Orders just came in, we're to fly out to New Orleans, and meet with Jinsu. He has some company he needs escorted back to Africa. We also need to make a stop in Chicago after." "Why?" Love asked as they reached the car. "Langley has a guy who's in need of a ride. Off the record. He said his name is Murphy." "I've never heard of him. But what of that other protection we discussed?" "It's being taken care of..." . . .

Ring, Ring, Ring... Ring, Ring, Ring. "This is Langley." He said answering the phone. The voice on the other end of the line cracked in, and out over the static. "Everything is in motion, Where are you on finding him?" Lucifer asked. Murphy had yet to call in, so Langley truly had no idea. But he wasn't about to tell Lucifer this. "All is well, my guy should be making contact with him soon. I'll contact you as soon as his line is open." "You do so Langley, and do so soon. Do not disappoint me." Lucifer replied with a cold, and forceful tone. "Yes sir. Everything is under control. But if I may ask my Lord. Is all of this really worth one man? Why is he so important?.." Langley asked, but there was no reply, only silence. "Sir.' Langley repeated, but still no answer. He looked down at the phone realizing the call had ended. Langley then slammed the phone down on his a cop. I'm a private investigator from Chicago." She looked over through the window then said, "This is me just up ahead on the right." Murphy didn't push. He just pulled the car up to the location she said. "I guess this is it?" He said as he put the car in park. "Well, thank you for the ride Mr. Murphy. If that is your real name." She said as she gathered her bags. "Yes, it is, and you can call me Kyle." She looked over at him, and could see the sincerity in his eyes. "Well sense we're being honest my name is Faith Hope." The words fell on Murphy's ears like the sound of cannons. "Well hold on a second." He said getting out of the car, and walking around to her side. "Let me help you with your bags." By this time Faith had totally forgotten about Sin waiting up stairs, as she allowed Murphy to help carry her bags up. As they made their way to the elevator they continued to talk. Murphy asked her questions concerning her love life, as she explained how there was no longer a man in her life. Once they were upstairs he followed her down the hall as she lead the way to her condo. "This is me here. Thank you for all your help." She said as she unlocked the door then opened it. "It's not a problem, but are you sure you'll be alright?" Murphy asked peering over her shoulder trying to gain a look inside. "Yeah, I'll be fine." Hearing the voices Sin had placed himself against the wall behind the door before it opened. "Well I guess this is it then. Um... Would it be alright if I left you with my number?" Murphy asked with a easy going smile. She smiled as she replied. "Just wait here a second. "I left my phone on the charger." After pushing the door up slightly closing it, she began walking to the back room. "Huuu.." A sudden gasp for air as a hand covered her mouth, and the arms of a man rapped around her from behind. "Shhh... Relax. Just calm down it's Sin." He whispered. Suddenly she had began to remember. "Oh my God." She thought to herself as he loosened his hold on her. "I hope you don't mind, I brought our bags in." Murphy said pausing as he walked in. "Oh, I'm sorry I didn't know you had company. I hope I'm not interrupting, forgive my intrusion." He said staring Sin directly in the eyes. "No, Kyle this is not what it seems. This is... My cousin, he just surprised me thats all. Let me just grab the phone." she said walking to the back room. "It's Kyle right?" Sin asked as he walked over extending his hand. Murphy took his hand with a firm grip, and replied. "It's Murphy.. You can call me Murphy, and you are?" Sin tightened his grip as he could feel Murphy squeezing his hand. Looking Murphy directly in the eye's he replied. "Sin.. You can call me Sin." And just like that, it begun.

Murphy pulled Sin forward taking his left hand, and landing a hook to Sin's jaw, causing him to stumble to the side. Murphy followed pressing against Sin's throat ramming him up against the wall. Releasing Sins hand Murphy tried for a right hook connecting with the side of Sin's head. He recoiled striking with the same hand, only this time being blocked as Sin through his left arm up in a guard. Crossing his right arm across the top of Murphy's, he pressed Murphy's arm down from off his neck, freeing himself from the choke hold. As his arm dropped Murphy countered with another right hook, accompanied by a left knee strike. He landed the hook, but was blocked on the knee as Sin dropped his forearm on top of it. Sin countered shoving Murphy in the chest creating space as he followed with a left front kick. As Murphy stumbled back Sin exploded forward leaping with a right superman punch. "Here it is." Faith said as she walked back into the room waving the phone in her hand. "Is everything alright?" She asked as she noticed the two men standing there still shaking hands. Never loosing each other gaze Murphy answered. "Yes of course. Everything's fine. It was nice to meet you Sin." He said as the battle in their minds had concluded. "Like wise." Sin replied releasing the grip on his hand. Murphy then continued to exchange information with Faith. Once they were finished he said his goodbye's, and began to leave. "Are you sure a long distance relationship is what your interested in?" Faith asked as Murphy walked out the door. "I travel a lot for work, so it's the only kind I know how to have." He said smiling as he replied, then closed the door behind him. "Who was that guy?" Sin asked as soon as he was gone? "I don't know, I just met him. He was nice though. He helped me out, and gave me a ride home after some guys wouldn't leave me alone. Why do you ask?" "No reason, I was just curious. Looks like he left his wallet, maybe if I run it out to him, I can catch him." I grabbed the wallet, and walked out of the door before she could reply. Once in the hallway I could see the elevator had yet to reach the bottom. It would take to much time to wait for it if I was going to catch him. So I took to the stairs, jumping 3 steps at a time as I rushed to the bottom. Pushing the exit door open I spotted Murphy leaving the lobby exit. I jogged through the lobby reaching the door where I noticed Murphy standing there, waiting against his car with his arms folded across his chest. I slowly walked over with the kitchen knife I grabbed pretending it was his wallet, comfortably hanging under my shirt sleeve incase he tried anything. "So who are you really Murphy? What ever this is, let's leave the girl out of this." I said as I drew closer. He dropped his arms, and reached for his waist line. I let the knife drop catching the end of the blade between my finger tips, ready to hurl the knife into his chest. "Easy there killer." He said raising his left hand as to say stop. He looked down at the blade then continued. "There's someone who wants to speak with you." He lifted his shirt showing the phone on his hip, as he slowly pulled the phone out, and pressed the speed dial. He then held the phone up in a gesture for me to come get it. "Put it on speaker." As you wish." He replied as he pressed the button. "This is Langley." The voice on the line answered. "Murphy, Are you there?" I walked over, and grabbed the phone. "This is Sin." I answered. "Sin, where the hell are you?" "It doesn't matter, you found me." "Where is Murphy?" "Alive, if that's what you mean." "Listen Sin, we need to get back on track. Head for the train station, and get down to New Orleans. I'll have a man meet you down there with all of your things." He said as if to give an order like he was really in control. Well I had some questions that need to be answered to. "What happened at the club Langley?" I replied coldly. "What do you mean?" "You know fucking well what I mean Langley! Did you try to have me killed?" I shouted trying to get control of myself. I could see Murphy

"Sir, everything is back on track, I found him." Langley said excited to break the news. "Do you wait for an applause Langley?" Lucifer asked. "No my Lord. I don't understand." "Do not seek praise, or approval for what you do, when all you've done was your job to began with. You do well Langley, and continue to. In time I shall make you a king." Those few words was all Langley needed to hear to know he was appreciated. "I've sent my guy to make arrangements for the new Soudi King. Love has gone with him to make sure the succession go's to him. How should we handle the standing King? Shall he pass the same as his predecessor?" "No. Let's strike a blow for the Shiite rebels. Send your man to Yemen, have him convince the prime minister it is in his best interest to resign rather than make further concessions to the rebels. This crisis will create a terrorism success story putting fear into the people. Now that the Sunnis allied with Al-Qaeda we can make the assassination appear as if they did it. I'm sure they will love to take claim for it. Although the Houthi rebels are anti American with slogans including Death to America, they are also sworn enemies of Al-Qaeda in the Arabian Peninsula. This is an opportunity to make our prince look like a hero in the war against them. And a progressive leader uniting enemies to combat a common enemy." "Are you sure the rebels will comply?" "Do not underestimate the ambitions, and greed of men Langley, it is how we keep control. All kings, and queens do not grow old in their reign without my help..." We walked into the train station, as I glanced around looking for anyone who could possibly be the contact. "Ms. Hope. Ms. Faith Hope please report to the security station." A voice said over the loud speaker. There was the contact I was looking for. "Listen Faith, you've done enough, and I can't ask you to go further." I told her not knowing what awaited me. And she was already in far enough. "So this is it then." She replied. "Looks that way, but I want you to wait here until I return. By chance I don't, I want you to take this information. Go to the address,and follow the instructions, I just want to say thanks for everything." I said then walked over to the security post. Where a heavy set Latino man stood out in front of the room. He opened the door, and waved me in as I walked over. "Hope?" He asked sarcastically. "It's Sin." I replied as I walked past him into the room. "Sin, you said?" A blond haired man sitting behind the desk asked. "That's correct." I replied. He stood up from behind the desk appearing to never stop growing, as I looked up his 6'9 frame. He lifted a black duffle bag, and sat it on the desk. "Take it. It belongs to you." He said keeping one hand rested on the butt of his gun. I opened the bag, and went through the contents it was indeed my bag, and everything was still in it, including a ticket set for midnight. "Is that all?" I asked. He nodded his head then took his seat, as I grabbed the bag,and walked out. "Faith!" I called over to where she was seated. She stood up as I walked over, and sat the bag on the armrest of the chair then opened it. "Listen, I want you to take this money, and start over." I said pulling a stack of $20 dollar bills worth a thousand dollars from the bag. "These day's that's not really a lot to start with, but I appreciate the offer." She said taking the money from my hand. "That money is for your travel expenses. I want you to use that information I gave you. It's up to you, but I think a better life is waiting for you outside of Miami." She stood there looking at me intensely as I packed up the bag. "I have to go now, but you remember what I said.'"I grabbed the bag then walked away heading for the train. I hopped she uses that information. Truth is I didn't think it was safe for her anymore, now that they knew who she was. But it wasn't my problem anymore, my part was done. It's all on her now, I'm headed to New Orleans.

Chapter 8

"We are approaching our destination. Please fasten all seat belts as we descend into our landing." The plane had landed on a private air strip in New orleans. As it made it's round the plane slowed near a hanger where a rolls royce sat parked out in front. As the door to the plane opened Jinsu exited the rear door of the black, and gray Bentley. "Hello Jinsu, long time no see!" Love yelled out standing in the door way of the plane. "5 decades, and you haven't aged a bit sense the day you signed over your soul to me. You seem to have done right for yourself. Are all your dreams coming true?" Jinsu asked. "You know the funny thing about getting everything you want Jinsu? Once you have it, you begin to desire for more." "A funny thing isn't it ?" Jinsu replied. "We have some time to kill while the planes being re-fueled, but your package will be safe with me." Love stated as she walked back inside the plane. Jinsu slapped the top of the car twice, and the other rear door opened. Exiting the car was the Saudi Prince brother to the king. The two men walked over to the steps of the plane then exchanged hand shakes. "Ugh!" The prince grunted as Jinsu swiftly slit his wrist while firmly gripping his hand. "Welcome aboard brotha." Jinsu said as the blood from the prince's wrist poured out covering the palms of their hands. The prince stood there his life pouring out of him as he continued to bleed out. The strangest thing was his body never grew weaker. "We have arranged for your National Guard, and Internal Security force to be trained by the United States as soon as you take power. They'll be largely equipped with everything you need." Jinsu stated releasing his hand as his wrist stopped bleeding. "Take care." He continued as he walked back to the Bentley. "Wheels up your highness." Aknubious said standing in the door way of the plane. "It's king Fahdull." The prince responded as he brushed passed Aknubious boarding the plane.

"In world news today. Ukrainian troops give up main airport terminal. Ukraine withdrew it's military forces from the main terminal of Donetsk Airport after months for fighting with pro- Russian separatists over the strategic facility. Fighting or the airport peaked over the weekend, shattering the relative tranquility since a new trust was reached in late December. Ukraine's President gave an emotional speech, and plea for help stating Russia as the aggressor in a conflict that has killed almost 5,000 people. More than 9,000 Russian troops entered the country with more than 500 tanks, armored personnel carriers, and heavy artillery units. Talks on ending the escalation in violence took place in Berlin over the weekend, but there was no breakthrough as off yet to achieve a peace accord."

Love laughed as she turned the t.v. off jumping into Aknubious arms. "You did it baby. Soon we can expand our reign all across Europe, and eventually the world." Love joyfully said as they sat back, and prepared for the plane to take off. . . .

"Welcome to the Taj Mahal." A young brown skinned Indian man greeted as the U.S President was escorted in by his secret service. "Sir you have an urgent call." The woman security officer told the president as she pulled out a satellite phone. "This is president Gainny." "Sir we have a problem. War has suddenly broken out in the Ukraine again. Their president is requesting an immediate audience with you concerning our aid." "I'm headed back to the plane now. Send over everything you have, I'll brief my staff, and we'll take it from there." The president responded as the security team escorted him from the building. "Some one get me Director Langley on the line." The president ordered as they entered the motor cage, and began heading for the private air strip where Air Force 1 was being held. "Sir." A secret service agent said as he handed the president a phone. "The line is secure sir." "Thank you. Hello." "This is Langley what in the world is going on? I thought this was under control already?" Sir remain calm, I'm on top of everything. As you leave New Delhi arrange for your flight to head to the vatican, he wants to see you. I'll arrange for the meeting with the Ukrainian President to br taken place there as well." Langley replied. "Do not worry sir, I'm on it." He continued then hung up the phone.

Doo, Doo... Doo, Dooo.... "Hello Langley." Love answered expecting the call. "Have you seen the news Love?" Langley asked not in the mood for being coy. "Is there a problem Langley?" She asked as if she was surprised at what was going on. "Your reign is the problem Love, it's out of control! Who authorized for them to do that?" "Do what exactly?" I haven't the slightest idea of what your referring to. I haven't been there in quite some time, handling your affairs!" She replied in an aggravated tone. "Well you find out what the fuck is going on over there, and handle it. Or we'll find someone who can." Langley said sternly then hung up. Love began to giggle as she tossed the phone down, and reclined in her seat. "You see Aknubious, a little chaos, and these boys loose control. To be a great king it takes a woman's touch." She said as she begun to drink a glass of wine. These were words that seemed to offend their passenger. Words the Saudi Prince could not agree with.

"I'm so fucking tired." Murphy thought to himself as he exited the redeye flight from Miami. He pulled the phone from his hip, switching it on as he walked through the terminal. 2 missed calls, and a message was showing on the display. The first call he recognized as Langley. But the second was a number he hadn't seen before. Murphy checked the message to see who had called. "Press 1 to play message. Hi this is Faith, I assume your still on the plane, but i remembered I didn't give you my number, anyway you have it now, if you still want to keep in touch Ok. Message ended." Murphy smiled at the thought as he prepared to return Langley's call. "This is Langley." "Go for Murphy." He replied. "Confirmed. Plans have changed Murphy, I need you to go into Yemen. I'm emailing you cryptic details to your assignment. You have 72 hours to complete. Once done, there is a woman whom you'll be traveling with, continue the original mission, and keep a close eye on her. Be on standby awaiting my call. And Murphy, there is a man she's traveling with. Stay clear of him if you can." "Understand." Murphy said as they disconnected the line. The email came in just as Langley said. The target; Yemen's Prime minister.

Murphy walked out of the airport searching for a cab, when a black limousine pulled in front of him. The limo tint made it impossible to see who was inside, when suddenly the back window rolled down. "You Murphy?" The deep voice of a man said from inside. "Who's asking?" Murphy replied. "I'm here on behalf of Langley." The man said giving Murphy some relief. Murphy knelt over looking into the window for a better look at the man's face. When his eyes were met by the sight of a woman knelt over with her face in the mans lap. The sun dress she wore was hiked up over her waist exposing the bareness of her light colored ass. As she reached underneath herself, stimulating her clitoris causing the moisture to drip down her fingers. She made the most seductive noises as she rolled her hips, stroking the shaft of his man hood with her other hand while sucking the head in her mouth. Murphy stood stunned for a moment as he watched Aknubious massage her exposed breasts. "Are you coming?" Aknubious asked. "Are you?" Murphy mumbled under his breath as he opened the door. Sliding pass them as he entered. He took a seat on the opposite end of the limo. Finding himself faced with the glow of Love ass, and the wet sight of her pussy as the moisture creamed down her legs. He couldn't help but think, what a beautiful sight as he became aroused. Love sat up as she climbed on to Aknubious lap, facing Murphy in a reverse cowgirl. She watched as the penetration hypnotized him. Gyrating her hips around as she bounced up, and down while rubbing her clitoris between her finger tips. "You don't to have just watch. You can have some." She moaned to Murphy as her hips continued to swirl. Hypnotized, Murphy began sliding his hand into pants, when he suddenly caught the cold dead eyes of Aknubious staring back at him. A look that told him, he wasn't welcomed. He snatched his hand from his penis then replied. :Maybe some other time." As he began to stare out the window. . . .

It had taken almost half a day, but I was finally in New Orleans. The train slowed as it pulled into the station coming to a stop. Picking up my bag I stood near the doors, and waited for them to open. My attention was drawn to a man whom appeared to be homeless as he walked among the people asking everyone for change. I reached in my pocket, and counted off 3 hundred dollar bills, then folded them in the palm of my hand as the doors opened. I walked out, and as I expected, the man made his way over to me. "Spare some change!" He asked as I extended my hand placing the bills in his palm. He never looked at the money as he closed his fist on mine, and stared into my face. "It's alright brother." I said trying to pull my hand away, but he continued to just stare at me. "Sin!" A voice called out to me from the distant. I turned to find a slender built caucasian man with icy blue eyes, wearing a two piece gray colored suit, under a black suede trench coat standing a few feet away. The homeless gentlemen looked over to the man, suddenly releasing my hand as he turned, and quickly walked away. "Do you like gospel music?" He asked as I walked over. "It's alright." "Good, the name Jinsu, and welcome to New Orleans." He led the way as he escorted me out of the station. "What is it you want?" He asked as we made our way to the parking lot. "I dont understand." "Sure you do. Everyone wants something in this world. It's what keeps us going." He said as we climbed in the back seat of his rolls royce. "So what keeps you going Mr. Sin?" I paused for a moment thinking about the question. "I just want my revenge." I stated. "And then what?" What will you do after you have it? What then will keep you going everyday, and why does it matter so much to you?" The question he asked had never occurred to me before. Something many of us never considered, and all I can say in response was.

"The job. I'll still have the job to do." But this time there was no response. He just leaned back in his seat as the car began to move. I did the same, leaning back in the seat as I turned, and stared out of the window. When my eyes were met by the eyes of the homeless man from the platform. His gaze continued to follow the car until we were no longer is sight anymore.

We road in silence as we crossed town, it gave me some time to reconsider the questions be asked. I was told I wouldn't age anymore, and how long can I really keep doing this? What else in life can I want, when I've been so blinded by revenge? I'm letting him fuck with my head, and I can't afford to let anyone in. The less I think about it, the easier it is to keep moving forward. "We're here." Jinsu said snapping me back to reality as the car came to a stop in front of a large church. Which was oddly strange to me. When your young you learn that demons, or devils weren't allowed inside of churches, which didn't come as a problem for Jinsu as we walked in. "You seem troubled?" He asked as we took a seat. There wasn't many people there at this time, but the few that were, sat quietly enjoying the sound of the choir, while others were deep in prayer. "I don't understand. How are we able to be here?" I asked, as he laughed then responded. "In the book of Job, God called all the sons of God to bear witness to his loyal servant, and Satan was there. You see, this is only a building, not Heaven. I am what you would call a cross roads demon, and this may not be a road, but there is a cross and the road is life. I come here to hear the prayers, and desires of man. From a new car, to political gain, fame, talent, a better job, a raise, and even to smite one's enemy. Then I give it to them, at a small cost of course. Nothing more than their loyalty, and soul. Something they didn't know what to do with to begin with." "What gain is there for you in that?" I asked. "You see, all things work together for the greatness of your God. We make a person desirable, and talented, then they use that to live the life they always wanted. And in return we use their influence to influence the masses in the way we want them to be. From artist who tell you to break all commandments, and politicians who make new one's for them to follow." He said with a proud smile on his face. "What gives you this power?" I asked. "Well I'm not just a demon, I'm a Jin." A cool chill came over me as I suddenly realize the extent a Jin's power can reach. I gathered myself then continued to ask. "Why then so many religions?" "Well, there is only one God, but in order to get man to except another. We had to first convince them that there was a different one, and at the same time teach them to be obedient in the way we want. People unite when there is a common enemy, then divide when they see each other as enemy's. It's easier to catch a calf when it is alone rather than when it is with the herd." "Why tell me all of this?" "Because you asked. What you have us an whew is opportunity to be apart of something great, and it's your choice if you want to be a prominent piece on the board, or just another pawn in the game. So I ask you again, What is it you really want?" I still had no answer for his question. "It's ok, take your time, just not to much." He continued as he stood up. "Now lets go." He proceeded to lead the way as we exited the church. As we walked down the steps I noticed a man standing across the street watching us as we walked o the car. I recognized this man. This was the same man from the train station. Who was he? "You coming?" Jinsu asked from inside the car as his driver held the door open. "Yeah, I'm coming."

"So tell me Sin. Do you happen to own a suit?" "Not at the moment, but why? Where are we headed?" "I'm going to take you to a place of mine, where you can shower, and get a little rest before the party." "What party?" I asked. "It's just an evening of entertaining some colleagues." "Well I appreciate the offer, but if there isn't a job for me to do, theres some other things I need to attend to." "I see, so let me be clear. That wasn't a request. I know exactly what you need to attend to." There was no need to reply. It was clear that there was nothing left to be said.

. . .

"Welcome home Mr. President, or do you prefer Minister Hadqren."

Murphy said as he turned the lights on. Startled to find someone in his home, the minister quickly turned around placing his back against the wall. "Who are you? And what are you doing in my house? What do you want? Guards! Where are my guards?" He yelled. Dressed as a Houthi rebel Murphy replied in the Arabic language. "They're of no use to you now." "What of my family? What have you done with them?" "That's entirely up to you Prime Minister..."

. . .

"Welcome President Enko." President Gainny said as he extended his hand. "Please, call me Vladislav. After today I hope we are able to call ourself's friends." "I have no doubt that we will." Gainny replied. "Good to hear. Shall we begin?" Enko responded as he shook Gainny's hand. The men began to walk down to a large door located at the end of a corridor accompanied by their security details. "The Vatican is such a lovely place, would you agree?" Enko asked as they came to the door. "Yes it is." Gainny replied. "Unfortunately this is as far as our security teams can go." He continued, "Yes, I understand." Enko complied. The two president's entered the room, and began their negotiations as they took a seat. "The problem we have is separatist leader Alexa Chenko, and the Kremlin are sticking to their story of who's responsible for the attacks, and Chenko is blaming Ukrainian government troops. But as we sit here looking for clarity, tensions in the region continues to rise." Gainny stated. "Yes, Mr. Gainny, they deny, but we have proof. One of our operatives, Vladimir Savchenko was on a rescue mission near Luhanask when his party was ambushed by pro- Russian separatist. Two days later he was handed over to Russian intelligence officers inside Ukraine then transferred across the border with a sack over his head." "The Russians are saying they were offering him asylum." Gainny interjected. "Yes, but you YouTube has uncovered video showing Savchenko in uniform, being interrogated by his captors inside Ukraine while handcuffed to a pipe. Not exactly someone fleeing persecution. He has now been charged with directing mortar fire that resulted in the deaths of two Russian journalist." "That is all very interesting Mr. President, but what are you going to do about it?" A voice said from shadows. "Who else is with us? I thought this was to be a private matter." Enko stated. "I assure you, I was never here, and this discussion never took place." The voice replied as a shadowy figure began to appear. "You are the pope." Enko said as the man entered the light. "Sometimes." The pope answered. "Now tell me, what is it you really want in life, Mr. President." He asked Enko as he continued. "I want peace for my country, and her people." "And what will you give for this. Your Soul?" If that is what it takes." Enko replied. The pope walked over to President Enko, then reached out his hand. "Then kiss the ring my son." As Enko did as he was told. He could feel the presence of his life force as if it was being drawn out of him. The pope then turned to walk out of the room. As he did, he looked over to President Gainny. "Well done my child. See to it he has what he needs." "Yes my Lord." Gainny replied as the pope exited the room.

Chapter 9

" In News tracking across the globe today. President Hadqren has been held captive in his home for over two days amid a standoff between powerful Iran backed Houthi rebels who control the capital. It is said the Houthi do not recognize the authority of parliament, because it consists of loyalist to Salleh. The Houthis have pressed for a reconstituted presidential commission to rule the country.

In other areas of the world the fighting continues between neighboring country's Russia, and Ukraine. We've received word that the U.S is now planning to place sanctions against Russia, as U.S troops prepare to deploy, and train Ukraine's National guard."

Dun, na, na Dun, na, na! "This just end we have more breaking news from Yemen. We're getting word that their president, prime minister, and cabinet has just resigned. The U.S Embassy remains open, and will operate as normal, although with reduced staff. The United States is reassessing the situation there. We'll have more on the development..."

I sat quietly on the bed listening to the news as I got out of the shower. I pressed the mute button so I could hear my own thoughts for a change. That proved to be rather hard with the sound of car doors opening then shutting as Jinsu's guest were arriving. People from all walks of life were in attendance. From Senators, Musicians, Models, and even the church pastor. I remembered the sign out front that read Pastor Diggons Ministry. In the distance beyond the tree's that lined the side walk, I noticed a man standing in what would have been a blind spot from anywhere else in the house. I threw on my clothes, and ran down stairs exiting through the side door. Trailing along the shadows of the property I managed to stay out of sight as I drew closer to where the man stood. Once I was near the curb I would have to walk out into the street light. Hopefully whatever he was watching kept his attention. As I slowly drew closer he suddenly began to walk away. "Hey!" I yelled out stepping into the light, but he continued to walk picking up his pace. I followed behind him in a light jog trying to bridge the gap in between us. He repeatedly glanced over his shoulder gauging our distance as he prepared to turn the corner. Just as he did I was able to catch a good glimpse of his face, recognizing him as the light illuminated around him. This was the same homeless man from before, had he been following us. But how? And why? "Hey!..Hey!" I yelled as he broke into a full sprint. "Hey..! I know you." I yelled, but he continued to run, and damn fast too. He cut across the street as I followed not watching where I was going. I bolted into the street catching the corner end of the front bumper on a blue Sedan that nearly ran me down. I stumbled to the ground, but was able to maintain my balance. I looked up just in time to notice him running into a opening between two houses. I quickly followed behind him continuing the chase. His feet were as light as feathers as he ran up a 7 foot brick wall and fell over. Picking up my speed I followed suit, one foot off the wall then I grabbed the top and pulled myself over. I wasn't about to loose him, or so I thought, until I was suddenly clothes lined in mid air as I came down. My body hit the ground hard but I was not ready yet to quit as I managed to grab his foot tripping him up as he tried to take off running. We rushed to our feet and the chase continued as he took off running through the parking lot of a Walmart. Whoever this man was, he didn't wanna be caught as he continued to weave between the cars. He ran up the back of a car diving over the roof of a van parked next to it. Rolling over the top then trying to cut back in the other direction. Coming over the van I was able to close the gap between us as I grabbed his shoulder from behind. Using his left he grabbed a hold of my hand, reaching back with his right arm rotating it around mine, and locking it in place. As he reverse kicked me in the ribs, causing my body to tighten from the blow. He then followed by slinging me forward through the front windshield of a parked car. He dragged me to the hood of the car placing me in a rear naked choke hold. "Who are you?" He asked as I struggled to get free. "Why did you go back Anoku?" My eyes widened hearing him call me by a name I hadn't heard in years. "Who..are..you?" I managed to cough out. "You don't remember." He said sounding surprised. As people begun to crowd I could hear the sound of police sirens coming in the distance. "There's no time to explain, my name is Celestial, remember it, and stay alive. I'll find you." He said before taking off again. I dragged myself to my feet as I rolled off the car gasping to catch my breath. He had the right idea, I needed to get the hell out of here.

. . .

Ring, Ring...Ring. "Hello." Faith answered in an irritated tone. "Have I caught you at a bad time?" Murphy asked. "I'm sorry, who is this?" "It's Kyle, I could call back if you'd like." "No, it's fine." Faith replied excited, realizing who it was. "I'm just busy at work, but I can take my break." She continued. "Well I'd hate to get you in trouble." "No it's fine, I am so tired anyways." :Maybe you could use a vacation. I know we barely know each other, but I just finished up a job, and I could use a get away with some good company." "Well I don't know. I mean your a nice guy and all, but I don't know if I should be going God knows where with you so soon. Besides I was thinking of visiting some family in California." She replied with a smile on her face. "Sounds fun; I mean if you'd like some company that is. "Murphy asked in a playful manner. "All available personnel please report to the E.R we have a code blue." The voice on the loud speaker blared through the hospital. "I'm sorry I have to get back to work, but I'll call you with my answer." "I'll be waiting." Murphy replied.

"Ok, I'll call you later." Faith said smiling as she hung up the phone, then rushed to the E.R.

"I find it so amusing when people think they can hold on to this lift, and still partake in another." Love said after ease dropping on Murphy conversation. "You know if you really care about her, you have to let her go. Given your life this could only end one of two ways, and both of them end's with her being hurt." She continued. "And what exactly does that mean? Is that a threat?" Murphy asked as he looked up from the phone with hostility in his voice. "Relax tiger, I'm only saying. There are some who may seek to hurt her just to get to you, or get to you and still hurt her, think about it." She said as she crossed her legs and took a sip of her drink. The thigh high slit in her dress exposed her legs as Murphy's eyes followed it down to a pare of gold ankle strapped designer heels. Finished with matching manicured toes that complemented her red dress. Murphy couldn't make sense of why he was so attracted to her, but he was. "We're here to do a job, not be friends. And I'd thank you to stay out of my personal affairs." Murphy said preparing the syringe filled with tetraodontidae toxin injecting it in the webbing between the toes of the former Saudi King. "Long live the King." Aknubiousa said as Murphy looked up only to be knocked unconscious. "Get him on the plane. We'll find out how much Langley really knows." . . .

"Mr. Sin, you look as if you've just survived a tornado." Jinsu said as Sin walked back into the house. "Sin, I'd like you to meet President Kem Ui of North Korea." He continued as the man extended his hand for me to shake. "Our friend here is a valuable asset to the organization. You see whenever people begin to think they don't need us anymore, they get a quick reminder from their enemies the importance of our assistance, and protection. Like the mortar bombing of South Korea, or terrorist crisis Boka Horrom in Nigeria. Now tell us, what kind of trouble have you gotten into." Jinsu said as a statement, that was more of a threat. "No trouble." I said trying to think of a response. "I went for a jog, and had a little mis-hap with a pair of German shepherds." I continued. "Forgive my rudeness, but if you don't mind. I'd like to go and get cleaned up, if that alright." Jinsu stared at me with an untrusting look then replied. "Of course." "It was nice meeting you." I said to the North Korean President, whom nodded his head as I walked out of the room.

"My Lord; My sources tell me that our Love has been double dealing. The attack on Ukraine was all her doing. I've also received information through our banking sources that there has been some talk of Russia joining the (EEC), and their joint currency. Making them a part of the European Union. If I must say my Lord." "Save it Langley, I am well aware of what this means." Lucifer interjected. "If Russia joins the EU, then claims Ukraine it will become to powerful. Able to also claim all of the smaller neighboring country's surrounding Ukraine, and eventually to large to stop. Claiming new leadership over the EU in one shared European Economic Community. She will have obtained all of Europe, this is eventually where we intended for things to go, but what troubles me is the fact that I was not informed first. I believe Mie Love's ambitions have grown too great." Langley listened to Lucifer as he paced back and forth in his office. He repeatedly pressed the re-dial button on a secondary phone which layed on the desk every time he walked past. "Sir I have another problem concerning the situation." Langley said continuing the conversation. "My guy who handled the Yemen arrangement. I placed him on standby next to Love incase you gave the order, but I've been unable to contact him. I'm humbly requesting you allow me to send a rescue team into retrieve him, before you send someone after her." "No. I have a better idea. I'll see to it you get your man back." "Yes, thank you Sir." Langley said as the phone went dead.

. . .

Doo, doo... Doo. "Hello brother." Jinsu said answering the phone. "How are things?" Lucifer asked. "As well as can be. What can I do for you?" "It's time we give sin a little present. Our brother Aknubious has decided to change allegiance, and seeks my thrown for themselves. Send Sin for him, and that little bitch Love." A stern and concentrating look came over Jinsu's face as he rebutted. "Are you sure he's ready for Aknibious?" "Make him ready!" "As you wish my Lord." Jinsu replied then ended the call.

· · ·

"Ahhh!" Murphy screamed out as Aknubious continued to torture him. "What were your orders concerning me?" Love asked as she prepared another branding iron over a fire. Murphy's body had been badly beaten as it gave up shivering from the cold, snowy Russian wilderness. His arms stretched behind him, high around a tree with his wrist tied together. His head hung in exhaustion, focusing whatever strength he had left to stand on the tips of his toes. He had to prevent his weight from dropping, and his shoulders from ripping out of their sockets. His toes were beginning to turn black as the frost bite from the snow set in. If Aknubious didn't kill him, surely hypothermia would. "Get him inside; I don't want him to die before he talks." Love said to Aknubious who then cut the restraints from Murphy's arms. Letting him fall to the ground as he took him by the foot and drug him inside. "Tomorrow we'll put him on the hook, maybe he'll talk then." "If not, maybe I'll go see that little girlfriend of his, and see what she knows." Love said loud enough for Murphy to hear as she used his phone to return Faiths text.

"American Airlines to Russia, flight 437 is now boarding." I could hear the voice of a woman calling my flight over the loud speaker of the airport. I stood in line at gate 13 watching all the busy people move to and from throughout the airport. "Thank you, have a nice flight." The stewardess checking tickets in front of the terminal repeatedly said as people continued to board. "Come with me." A man said as he suddenly walked up behind me. He looked familiar, but I didn't know where I recognize him from. "Who are you?" "It's me Celestial." He said looking un recognizable after cleaning himself up. "How do you know me?" I asked whispering as people began watching us. "I'll explain everything if you'll come with me." He replied in a low tone. "Not now, I'm to close." I said fighting my curiosity. "Well if you want come, then I'm coming with you." Celestial replied pulling out a plane ticket from his inner coat pocket. How do you even know where I'm Going?" "I don't, but I was 3 people behind you in line when you got your ticket. And I know you're going to Moscow." He said as we approached the stewardess handing her our tickets. "You gentlemen will be seated in first class. It's to your left when you enter the plane." "Look what do you want from me?" I asked as we boarded the plane. "I was there when you decided to walk away, don't you remember?" He said as if I should. "I think you have me confused with someone else." "Then how do I know your name is Anoku?" "That was my fathers name also, maybe you knew him. But I didn't my name is Sin." "Anoku, you are your father, and your true name is Annunaki." "What is that? Some kind of cliche." "No brotha." He said pulling his dreads into a pony tail. "I was there when we took the fall from Heaven. I was there when we were good soldiers helping Lucifer build this world. And I was there when you finally had enough, when the regret became too much for you. Don't you remember?" We had a plan to start over and return to Heaven. You chose that woman to bestow your essence into, giving birth to a new life. A life that could go to Heaven when you died. But now you've returned, what happened?" I didn't know what to make of all of this. If indeed all that he had said was true, which wasn't hard to believe given my current situation. What does it all mean?" "Celestial, if this is true, why did you leave me?" "Because." He took a moment to gather himself then proceeded. "I was the Jin assigned to bring you back. And once I didn't another was assigned to a Jin again." He replied. "But why?" "It was the least I could do, if you're going to go through with this. But understand, I was once a soul reaper; all souls must go somewhere, either Heaven or Hell. Since we can't return to heaven we only take them to one place, unless you bound them to yourself the same way I passed my grace on to you. These souls will give you power, but beware of the souls you keep. Darker souls have away of influencing you, making you lust for blood. You must maintain a balance unless you become like them. If that starts to happen, release those souls to hell or take more innocent ones in. This is really the only way you can become strong enough to stop a Jin, and they won't go easy." "I understand, but what of you?" "If I survive this trip with you, I plan to live out the rest of my days until it's done. Now let's get some rest." Celestial said leaning his seat back then turned off the over head light. I decided to do the same, but falling asleep wasn't something I wanted to deal with on a plane. "One more thing Celestial, what happens to the souls I keep if I die?" "They go where you go, as they are bound to you." "But what if the person was still alive, and I took their soul then died?" "I don't know, they may not die with you, but one thing for sure, when they do die they will join you wherever you are." "And just how many souls can I hold?" "As many as you can handle. You'll know when there's too much." "How about an army?" He looked over to me and laughed. "Maybe, I've never tried." He then replied, as he closed his eyes. "Listen, when we get there, you go ahead and I'll follow. Whoever you have to meet I don't need them to see me." There was nothing more he needed to say, for I understood his concern.

Once we reached Moscow I did as Celestial asked and went ahead. I exited the terminal where I was met by a woman that introduced herself as one of Langley's assets. She began explaining the task, and how it wasn't going to be easy, as we made our way to the car, then headed for the safe house. She told me that Love was held up in a compound outside of town. I looked through the file she was carrying which contained photographs of Loves location. The compound looked more like a modern day castle surrounded by acres of wilderness, and heavily guarded with soldiers. "How exactly was I suppose to get in here alone?" "That's not my concern. I was told to only prepare you with everything you need. Truth be told, if your going to have any shot at this target, it's best to go alone, and be quiet. You go in there with a team and storm the castle, she'll be gone before you could reach her." She said as we pulled into the garage of an old warehouse. Not the most comfortable safe house, but one thing for sure no one would come looking for us here." And here you are, everything you'll need is in here, good luck." She said as I got out of the car. She then backed out of the garage leaving me there. I looked around surveying the warehouse to find an old suburban truck, and a long steel table covered with arsenal of various weapons. What a variety to choose from, but there was no way I could carry it all. I began checking the hardware when I heard a loud knock coming from the side exit. I grabbed the MK9 jamming the magazine inside, then released the slide. "Doom, Doom!" Two quick knocks repeated as I approached the door. Pressing the release latch with my foot, I kept the gun pointed at dead center. "You still want my help, or have you decided to kill me?" Celestial said standing in the door way as the door opened. "How did you get here? Are you sure you weren't spotted?" I asked lowering the gun. "I've spent centuries tracking people, and reaping souls, this is not difficult." He said letting the door close behind him as he walked in. We walked over to the table where I exchanged the MK9 for a .223 assault riffle with a scope and suppressor. I grabbed a couple of extra magazines, a pare of hunting knives, and a suppressed .40 caliber glock 19. "Grab what what you need, our time table has been pushed up." I said placing the leg strap and holster on my right leg, then placing the glock into it. I put the two knives in the sheaths on the back of my waist band. Then I placed the .223 in the back seat of the truck, then started the engine. "We have about an hours drive, we should get moving." I said as Celestial placed a high powered snippers rifle on the rear seat, along with a bag of magazines. "Is that all you're taking?" "Yeah, and these." He replied throwing two snow white hooded trench coats over the bag. "Ahhh! My head." I yelled grabbing my head as millions of images began to bombard my m ind. "What is this? What is happening?" "It's my memories; there starting to take effect." Celestial spoke up. "Whenever you hold on to a soul you absorb all of it's memories and skills. You know everything they've ever known." "Why does it hurt? Is it always like this?" "No, but your mind is trying to adapt to centuries of memories. After this you should be able to handle any other soul, unless it is tormented, then you will have to adjust to what you're witnessing." The pain was beginning to subside as he continued to talk. "How are you feeling?" He asked without any concern, as he sat in the front passenger seat. His lack of concern actually put me at ease as it mad me know I'd be alright. "Better." I replied climbing into the driver seat of the truck. "You ready?" I asked. He nodded his head in conformation, and we were off.

We had drove for at least 45 minutes in silence when Celestial suddenly spoke. "You should have gotten some rest." The remark surprised me, but I replied. "I feel fine, why the concern?" He continued to stare out of the window as if he was deeply focused on something outside of it. Never looking away he answered. "You're going to need to be at your best." "I'm fine, but listen. We're about 25 minutes out till E.T.A. I've been going over the schematics in my head. There is a road coming up soon that will take us to the far northeast side of the compound at least half a mile away. It would take us roughly 15 minutes off course, but I figure we could use the heavy cover of the trees to gain closer access. It's less guarded and there a lower level entrance to the basement. That will be the point of entry." "I agree; I to have already considered the option." Then it was settled. We returned to silence as our turn off came up. I couldn't tell if Celestial was actually worried or just really focused. But one thing for sure, there was no turning back now.

. . .

"Bring me the prisoner, it's time we stop taking it light on him. This time I really want you to break him." Love demanded feeling frustrated from the lack of information Murphy was giving them. "Our physicians are seeing to him now. You push him anymore and he'll die, then we'll get nothing." Aknubious stated. "Then I think it's time we return to the states, and find that little girlfriend of his." "Lets first focus on the task at hand. Theres an incoming storm so there will be no flights till tomorrow. In the mean time we need to strike again at Ukraine while their still weak." "As you wish." Love replied picking up the phone on the office desk. "Hello." "Make it happen. "Right away ma'am." A few words was all that was needed, and soon after mortar shells would be dropping over Ukraine.

. . .

"Huuu, Huuu, Huu." I took in deep breaths trying to gain composure as we reached the trees on the edge of the compound, after tracking through the heavy snow. The snow white trench coats provided us with excellent camouflage in the snow. "Alright Sin, this is as far as I go." Celestial said as he bunkered down into the snow taking cover behind a tree. "What are you saying?" "I'm saying I'll take position here. I'll cover you going in, and wait to cover you coming out, but I can't go in with you." This had changed my plans, but I couldn't ask him for anymore then what he has already done. "Ok, you take out the patrolling guards, more specifically the gunners on the roof." "Not a problem; and Sin, if you find yourself in trouble in there. Make your way to this side of the building and I'll cover you as best I can through the windows." "Good to know. So what's your best guess to their locations?" "It beats me, but there is one way for you to know for sure." "And what is that?" "take the soul of someone who do" "Well, thanks for everything." I said then began running across the snow. "Tuff!" I took a knee in the snow as the muffled spit of a snipers rifle went off. "Thum!" The body of a man fell from he roof disappearing in the snow as it hit the ground. I gave a thumbs up to Celestial for good had to be dead, and there was no sound of anyone else coming. I slowly moved down the hall then checked the body before continuing on. The kill was confirmed and I was still undetected. I approached the door of a room where I believed the woman, and man should be located. I cracked the door and took a peek inside, but I could only see the man. He seemed to be just standing there staring at something. I pushed the door open a little further, just enough to get a clear shot but not enough to be noticed. When I finally got a glimpse of the woman, whom was down on her knees at the mans feet performing oral sex. "Thuph… Ummm! Thuph!" The first shot cutting his penis completely off, followed by a second shot to the head preventing him from screaming. "Ummm! Ummm!" The woman continued to try and scream, but was gagged by the mans severed penis still in her mouth. So scared and distraught she never thought to take it out. "Thuph!" A single shot to the forehead causing her body to hurl back as she died motionless on the floor. The woman seemed so out of place to me, so much I became curious to know what she knew. Without giving it any thought, I layed my hand on her chest, and suddenly it began glowing. Just as before, here soul passed onto me and I knew everything about her. She was a doctor, here caring for a patient. To my surprise that patient was Murphy, and that pretty boy face had surely seen some better days. His location wasn't far from where I was. I didn't know how much help he could be in his condition, but there was only one way to find out. I began making my way down the halls, clearing every corner before moving on. Oddly enough there seemed to be more guards outside then there was in here. Just ahead in the next room over is where Murphy was being held. Two guards stood outside of the door, both wearing body armor. I checked the slide and magazine of the glock. Two rounds left, then I would have to reload. Placing the glock in it's holster I then took off the .223, and checked the magazine. 11 rounds until I'll need to reload. I fired a round passed the guards ricocheting off the wall at the end of the hall. Drawing their attention as I leaped out, running toward them. Hearing my foot steps the men suddenly turned around. I took off sliding on my back, feet first across the tiled floor. Striking the first man with a kick to the knee, shattering it as it dislocated. "Tuff!" Firing form the ground the single shot from the .223 tore through the second's man head. Painting the ceiling as the bullet entered under his chin, and exited the top of his head. taking the butt of the rifle I struck devastating blow to the forehead of the first guard knocking him unconscious. after stripping him of his body armor I went ahead and broke his neck., snapping it in two places. I could see what Celestial meant. After every kill I yearned for more, each more violent than the last. I pushed the door open to find Murphy chained to a chair, unconscious and badly beaten. "Murphy.. Slap! Murphy! Wake up damn it... Slap!" I continued to try and slap him out of it to no avail. Looking over to what appeared to be an operating table accompanied by a silver tray with various devices for torture and syringe with a label that read, Adrenaline. Taking the syringe I jammed it into Murphy's chest forcefully, trying to bypass his chest muscles and rib cage, penetrating his heart. "Hu, Hu, Hu... Ahhh!" Murphy roared as the adrenaline surged through his veins waking him up. "Shhhh, shut the fuck up." I whispered covering Murphy's mouth with my hand. Having the doctors knowledge had come in handy. I now know things about the human body that a man in my profession should and shouldn't know. And I was itching to carve open Love's chest and leave a grenade in her heartless cavity. "Murphy you have to relax." He looked into my eyes with an intense stare as I begun to release his mouth. "Has Langley sent you for me?" "I guess you could say that." I replied while untieing his shackles. "Well I can't leave yet." "I see, but you're in pretty bad shape to be fighting." Relocate my shoulder then give me a gun. If you want to leave thats your choice." I took Murphy by the arm and prepared to reset it. "Alright brace yourself." "I'm Ahhhh!" Before he could finish his sentence his shoulder was back in place. I took out a magazine and reloaded my side arm. "With your shoulder the way it is, you wouldn't be able to handle anything more." I said handing him the direction as I took to my knee, haling his companion over my shoulders for cover. I took off running using the man as a shield, as Murphy leaped out taking the right flank picking off the other gun men. "Sin!" He yelled. "I'm clear." I responded dropping the man who had just taken nearly 30 rounds for me. I walked over and picked up my rifle then reloaded. "Check them for ammo." I said covering Murphy as I secured the area. "Two mags, 7 rounds each and I have one in the chamber." Murphy stated. I was now down to two magazines myself, so I thought it best to strip the dead guard of his side arm. A .9 millimeter Bereta, with only the magazine that was in it. At least it was good for another 15 rounds. "How you holding up?" "I'm fine." Murphy replied while acquiring another handgun from off the dead guards. "Let's use the suppressors to our advantage until we can't anymore. Then things will get loud giving away our positions, so make each shot count." "Agreed, but what the hell are you doing? This is no time to mourn or pray over their lost." Murphy replied as I took one of the men by the arm. "Just keep look out, and cover me." I replied as I reaped the mans soul. "So which way do we go? There has to be some other stairs leading to the next level." "We go this way." I stated taking lead down the hall. "How do you know? What if we're going the wrong way?" "We're not, I was given intel on the layout before I came. So be on your guard, there's at least 9 more soldiers on this level, and I don't know where they are." I whispered as we made our way down the hall, clearing each room as we went. "Quite…just wait." I said holding up my hand to halt as I listened intensely. "What did you hear?" "Quiet." I said stopping him as Murphy tried to whisper the question. Bop, bop bop,bop,bop,bop,bop! "Shit!" I mule kicked back knocking Murphy down as I dove to the ground. The bullets from the gatlin gun continued to rip through the wall one after the other grazing me as I was pined down. "Fu….ck!" I yelled returning fire through the wall until the gun was empty. There was no way I could get up without getting ripped to shreds. "Get out!" I screamed to Murphy. He scrambled to his feet firing off a few rounds drawing gunfire in his direction as he darted around a corner into a open hallway. I took the window of opportunity he had just given me. Jamming in the final magazine of the .223, as I jumped to my feet releasing the slide, chambering the first round. Tuff, Tuff, Tuff, Tuff… Tuff, Tuff! I opened fire running in the opposite direction of Murphy. Everything became as slow motion as my eye's met the eye's of the gun men. I stared through the gaping hole created by the gatlin gun where a wall had once been. "Aknubious ." I thought to myself continuing to fire as he turned his attention to me. At the end of the hall was a closed door. There was nowhere else to go, and no time to open it. I began running harder, picking up speed. Brock! I dove shoulder first bulldozing the door off it's hinges as I slid across the floor of the room.

Murphy made his way down the hall looking for a way to flank the gatlin gun. Releasing the empty mag from the gun he found himself suddenly ambushed before he could reload. Another man appeared into the hallway exiting a side door. Before the man could fully enter Murphy sprang into action. Hurling the gun into the mans face as he charged forward. Grabbing the barrel of the mans rifle and chopping him in the throat, followed with a kick to the solar plexus knocking the man back into the room. Causing the mens finger to tighten around the trigger as the gun began shooting into the air, catching one of the other men waiting in the room with a stray bullet to the head. Murphy drew the Bereta from his waist putting 4 slugs into the man's chest. After making sure the room was clear, he picked up the glock then reloaded it. "You know you won't be leaving here alive Annunaki, or is it Sin now?" Aknubious spoke out loud. As I listened I could hear his foot steps circling in on my position. I took better position behind a pool table setting my sight on the door way. "How about we just come out, and get this over with?" Tuff, Tuff! Two shots went into the wall next to the door. I knew there was only one way to this room, and he had to come down the hall to get to it. But there was no response, I'd hoped he would fire back giving up his position. "You got me Sin, I'm wounded." His voice continued to echo through out the room. I had no time to check the entire room, so it was possible there could be another entrance. I backed away from the pool table preparing to take cover behind the bar. "Bloom, Bloom, Bloom!" I ducked down behind a sofa as bottles and glasses of alcohol shattered on the bar. "Bloom, Bloom!" Two more shots ripped through the sofa as fethers from the exploding pillows fell over head. I jumped up to return fire, when I was met by Aknubious flying knee coming over the couch.

"Uhhh.." Stumbling back I dropped the gun crashing into a dresser. Aknubious landed on the other side of the couch charging towards me. The 5 shot 50 caliber revolver was clearly out of ammo as he tried to jam it into my face like a knife. I perryed to the right setting up to counter. Rib, throat rib, diaphragm, upper cut. Landing a solid quick 5 hit combo, causing him to stumble back. I looked for the finish trying to knock him off balance with an over hand left elbow, only to have it caught. He followed with a knee to my stomach, causing my body to curl over as he lifted me into a power bomb slinging me over his head and across the room. I could feel the pain of a fractured rib surging through my back as my body crashed through a table. Once again he was on the charge, I hopped to my feet, then rolled out of the way as he leaped forward with two quick front kicks. Back on my feet we now began to square each other off. He flenched deciding to make the first move. Faking with a foot sweep he leaped forward with a half superman punch, into a high left kick, followed by two jabs then a knee.

The combination of his flurry was powerful as I tried to match with counters. First perrying outside of the superman punch, then a high right arm block protecting my head, with a mid left arm guard shielding my ribs from the kick. His strikes was so powerful it caused me to stumble a bit, as I prepared for the following jabs. Side stepping the first one, I followed with a duck to the outside of the second, into a low block catching the knee. Immediately turning my hand over into a reverse palm strike

I landed a blow to the diaphragm. Knocking the air out of him, but not slowing him down, as he countered with a head buck.

Murphy waited along side a wall, awaiting the 3 guards approaching his position. The barrel of the first mans rifle appeared as he entered the room. With both guns in hand, Murphy knocked the barrel of the rifle up taking his pistol, and repeatedly jamming it into the mans face as he charged him into his accomplices, running the 3 men into the hall as he opened fire through the mans face. "Thuff, Thuff, Thuff, Thuph." The repeated rounds from the .40 caliber ripped through the heads of the first and second man hitting the third in the throat. "Yeah!.. Woo!" Murphy yelled in triumph, then made his way back to find Sin.

"Come on." I continued to tell myself. Trying to focus as Aknubious seemed to be getting the upper hand over me. We exchanged blows, strike after strike, but for everyone of my strikes it felt like he was landing two, to three more. "Ouuu." I grunted as the strong grip of his hand lodged around my neck. I drew the bereta from my waist firing off a shot through his side, then another that grazed off the edge of his jaw bone.He released my neck striking me in the face with the same hand, then reached for the gun. Twisting my arm to the inside he prepared to break it. I spun with a reverse elbow strike putting more strain on my twisted shoulder, but cutting him across the brow. I dropped forward taking to one knee as I dropped the bereta catching it in my left hand. "Bou! Bou!" Two shots, one ripping into his thigh the other grazing him as he fell to his knee. I lifted the gun to his face just as he grabbed my wrist. "Bou! Bou! Bou!" I continued firing nearly missing as he wrestled to keep the gun away from his head. "Bou! Bou! Bou! Bou! Bou!" He shifted his weight after the last shot, allowing the force of my body to throw me off balance. Releasing my wrist as the gun swung past him, Aknubious followed with a devastating right hook across my left temple, dazing me as my ears began ringing. But the behemoth wasn't done yet. As he shoved me over mounting on top of me, delivering repeated elbow strikes, dropping all of his weight on me.

It was only a matter of time before I was unconscious. I could see him sit up through my blood stained eye's, as his fist began to barrage my face one after the other. My head bouncing off the ground as he attempted to beat me to death.

"Bou! Thuff! Bou! Bou! Thuff! Bou! Thuff!" The sounds of gun fire echoed as shards of glass and broken vases ricocheted everywhere. Aknubiousa dashed to his feet, darting through another exit as bullets wiped by him. Murphy ran into the room continuing the assault until Aknubious was no longer in sight, and both guns were empty. "You still alive?" Murphy asked taking the berets from my hand as I laid there covered in blood. "I'm fine. Get my gun, it's behind the couch." I could feel myself healing a lot faster as my strength returned to me. I rolled to my side bracing myself as I got up. I gave no attempt of wiping the blood away and revealing my wounds were healing as Murphy walked over handing me the gun. "You ready?" "Yeah, lets go." I replied as we followed Aknubious trail through another exit, locating a second stair well. Murphy took lead up the steps as I covered the rear. "Pouuu!" The loud echoing sound of a 12 gauge shotgun caught Murphy square in the chest, sending us flying down the stair case as I tried to catch him. My body crashed onto the floor at the base of the steps with Murphy landing on top of me. I raised the .223 as two men approached the top of the stairs. Bursting quick rapid fire in their direction. I was able to cut them down. "Click!" The gun went empty just as a third man appeared. My first instinct was to use Murphy as a shield. I hadn't had time to check if he was dead or unconscious, nor the condition of his body armor and how much more it can take. but if he wasn't already gone, I wasn't going to let him go out like this.

The man pointed his rifle as I rolled us over shielding murphy as I reached for his bereta. "Pow! Pow!" The man opened fire catching me twice in the back. "Ouuuu!" I screamed grabbing a hold of Murphy as I drug him off. "Thanks." Murphy whispered looking up at me, then fell unconscious. I had come too far to fail now. Grabbing two pool balls off the table, I then took position along the way at the base of the stairs. I hurled the two balls near the top of the steps. They began to thump sounding like rushing foot steps as they rolled down the steps. The man came to the edge of the stairs and fired a few rounds, stopping as he realized no-one was there. "Blou! Blou! Blou!I sprung from around the corner firing three rounds, two into his chest, and the third finding his cheek. I grabbed one of the pool balls and charged up the stairs. Third step from the top, I dove into the room rolling off of the floor into a full sprint as bullets zipped pass me. I blindly returned fire as I ran, sliding into a bathroom. I was now concerned, but far from done. Any moment now they would shoot this room into shreds, and then they're coming in for a body. I grabbed the straight razor off the bathroom sink, and a long towel from the shower rail. I could hear them gathering outside the door, maybe two or three people. I placed the pool ball in the towel, then jumped in the tub for cover. There was no more than three rounds left in the gun. "Plou! Plou! Plou! Plou! Plou!" Machine gun fire ripped through the door ricocheting throughout the room. I stayed down curled in the tub until the shooting stopped. Once I heard the door break open, I sprung up dropping the first man through with three rounds to the chest. I ducked back into the tub as the assault of bullets continued. "Click, click… clack." The sound of a empty magazine sliding out was my cue, the sounding of round 2. I leaped out of the tub spinning the towel around, then hurled it across the room like a slingshot, crashing the pool ball into the mans forehead, possibly killing him as he laid motionless. "Clap, Clap, Clap!" A slow applause sounded from the other room as Aknubious walked into view slamming his hands together. "Well done." He said sarcastically I glanced down to the gun laying at my feet. "Come now Sin, I don't think we need those anymore, do we?" He continued, drawing a handgun from the rear of his waist. "Step away from it." I kicked the gun away, then flipped the blade of the straight razor out. "Now that's better." Aknubious knees and elbows. But the blows from Aknubious was starting to take a toll on him. Murphy swung a hard haymaker missing, causing his body to over extend. Aknubious quickly moved to the side delivering a crushing upper cut to his stomach. Murphy's body curled over and Aknubious quickly rolled him up into a power bomb. The floor cracked as Murphy's body slammed onto it. I scrambled to my feet as Murphy attempted to lock in a triangle. I rushed in just as Aknubiousa swung Murphy's body against the wall, then lifted him high above his head for a super power bomb, that would surely kill him. Diving across the room as hard as I could; I tracked Aknubious legs from behind, causing him to fall back with Murphy onto of him. I pulled the glass from my hand freeing it to heal for more mobility. Aknubious had quickly tossed Murphy off of him as he jumped to his feet charging toward me. He swung with a furious jab blowing past me, as I side stepped out of the way catching him with a uppercut, then a over hand jab of my own. Seeing him stumble Murphy followed crashing a bar stool over the back of his head. I quickly answered with a front stomp kick shattering his knee cap, then followed with a left hook to his chin as he buckled. Aknubious burst up from the ground lifting me into a sidewalk slam, as Murphy grabbed a vase from a dresser superman leaping across the room shattering the vase across Aknubious face. I glanced through the window as I caught the glair of a sniper scope high up in the tree's. I rolled over dragging Murphy to the ground as the sniper rounds tore through the window cutting Aknubious to pieces. Bullets ripped through his chest and head as his body flung up against the wall then dropped. As the shooting stopped I glanced outside barely able to make out Celestial in his white coat along the snow tree branches. I looked over to Murphy who was still laying on the floor, and noticed a large amount of blood. He laid there bleeding from a gunshot wound; I hadn't got to him in time, as one of thee sniper rounds pierced his lungs. He began to spit up blood as he tried to talk. "Save your words, and listen to me Murphy. I can save you, but you have to will fully give your soul." He laid there eyes squinted, looking at me like I was out of my damn mind. "She's going after Faith; don't let her get to her." He replied. "Over here!" I could hear a dozen men filling the room beneath me. I grabbed the two rifles from the dead guards along with Aknubious pistol. I opened fire down the steps emptying the clip to keep them at bay, then handed the other one to Murphy. I grabbed Aknubious body and dragged it to the window. Celestial must have known what I was about to do, as he began to open fire on the men below clearing a path. I gave one last look at Murphy as he proped himself up next to the stairwell. Keeping pressure on his wound. I kicked Aknubious body out of the window, riding his back into the snow. The impact of the fall still shocked my body, but nothing broke as his body absorbed most of it. I jumped to my feet sprinting across the snow with gun in hand as Celestial covered me. "What the hell are you doing Sin?" Celestial thought to himself as he continued to fire covering Sin. He began to detour from the path to the trees, firing rounds at the men approaching on snow mobiles. Sin gunned down two men hopping on their vehicle, and floored it back to where Celestial was. "Get on!" Sin yelled as Celestial slid down the tree. "Let's move." Celestial said as he hopped on the back. The snow jumped around them as bullets wized by knocking bark from the trees. We pushed through the woods at full throttle all the way back to the truck. "Sin, you're bleeding pretty bad." Celestial yelled over the motor. "I know, I took two shots in the back that didn't go straight through. Their lodged in there pretty deep, making it hard for the wounds to heal." Sin replied sweating profusely. "The roads just aheee…" Before he could complete his sentence, Sin had passed out, falling from the snow mobile as Celestial grabbed a hold of him. He drifted in and out of consciousness watching Celestials boots track in and out of the snow, before blacking out again.

Chapter 10

"Ring, ring Rin.." "What is it I can do for you Jinsu?" Lucifer asked answering the phone. "It's not what you could do for me my Lord. but rather what I can do for us." "Speak then Jinsu, without any delay." "It seems sins mission was a bit of success. Although Love managed to get away, Aknubious on the other hand can be credited as a big feat for him. But it seems he had some help getting out of there. Our dear Sin seems to have alined himself with an old friend, and wanted man." "Celestial." Lucifer interrupted. "Good work Jinsu; as always. Let us see where his loyalty truly lies."

. . .

"Ahhhhh! Shut the fuck up!" Murphy yelled through the darkness. "That's some temper you have there." Lucifer replied as he emerged from the shadows. The screams of the plagued souls quieted as the light illuminating from Lucifers silhouette drew closer. "Where in the hell am I? And who the fuck are you?" "You're home for the time being, and I? Well you can call me father.

. . .

When I awoke, to my surprise I found myself back inside the warehouse. I laid there on a cold steel table staring at the operating tray next to me. Celestial was nowhere insight. The truck was gone and it seemed I was stranded for the moment. My body trembled from the bitter cold of Russia's icy winter, turning the warehouse into an icebox. "Hunk! Hunk!" A horn sounded outside the garage door before it began to open. I quickly rolled off the table running to the arsenal of weapons across from me, then knelt behind the table. As the car pulled in I noticed the driver was the same woman whom had brought me here from the airport. "Hello." She said looking at my bare chest as I walked out. "You wouldn't happen to have some clothes for me, would you?" I asked as she stepped out of the car. "Right this way." She suductively replied as she led the way to a room that looked to had been an office once upon a time. She opened a locker that held a few pairs of men garments and a pair of jackets. "Where did your friend go?" I paused wondering who she could possibly be talking about. I was certain Celestial wouldn't have run the risk of being seen, even if I was dying. "What friend?" I answered. "You know, the one who brought you here, and patched you up." "What makes you think I didn't get here on my own, and fix myself?" Hearing the suspicion in my voice she began to change her tone and pointed out the obvious. "Well, the truck is gone, and your wounds appear to be in your back." My wounds may not have been completely healed, but in all this time they would be enough, not to warrant surgery. So what angle was she playing at? "They are, but do they look to be in need of surgery?" I asked turning to face her as I pulled on a sweater. "Well no, but someone sure did.Besides Langley said you should be accompanied by a man named Murphy." She stated bringing images of my last memory of him to the front of my mind. Damn...

. . .

"Ring, Ring... Ring, Ring... Ring, Ring." "Go ahead Langley." "I don't mean to bother you sir. But is there any word from Sin?" "His mission wasn't a total success but not a complete failure either." Lucifer stated leaving Langley on the edge of his seat. "Why not say what you really want to know? like what is the condition of your man." "Well yes of course sir.

93

But also the success of the mission as well, I know how important it is to the cause." "Cut the shit Langley, Your man is in good hands. He's being taken care of as we speak." "Thank you sir, again I'm sorry to bother you." Langley replied then hung up the phone. The full details was not clear to him yet, but as he seen it; this was a win-win situation. He would get his man back, and in the process knock off either Sin, Love or Aknubious. "Charles; what time is my United meeting with Canada, and Mexico's Presidents?" Langley asked pressing the intercom button on his desk. "Mexico's President should be landing shortly at your private landing strip. The plane should be refueled and ready to go by the time you get there. The Canadian president landed this morning and is awaiting your arrival." "Thank you Charles. Have the chopper ready in five. I'm leaving now." Langley replied pulling on his jacket. "Right away Sir."

. . .

"Doo, Doo, Doo.. Doo, Doo, Doo." My phone began to ring from the other room interrupting my thoughts. As well as our conversation as I rushed to answer it. "Go ahead." The static on the line told me exactly who it was. "I hope you're well rested, I have a job for you. Check your messages." Lucifer said, just as the phone began to vibrate; signaling a file was received. I clicked on the file, and a large picture covered the screen. It was Celestial. "Who is he?" I asked as if I hadn't already known. "Your mission." Lucifer replied. "Where do I find him?" "His location is not yet known, but he may just come after you. If you see him do not hesitate to send him home. It's been so long since we've said hello." "But why would he come for me?" "We've been hunting him for some time now, and he's been known to track down our hunters and kill them before they get to him. He's dangerous and may be studying you right now." "I understand." I replied finding it odd that he was willing to explain, as if he really wanted to convince me. "Your escort will take you to a ferry that will take you across to Nome, Alaska. You can make your way back to California from there." He continued before abruptly hanging up the phone. I looked over my shoulder to the woman. "I take it you're my escort? Well let's get a move on it."

. . .

"A work of art I must say. There is just enough humanity left in you to allow you to function in society, but your heart and mind is almost as cold as mine. Sun of sun, I think you're ready my son. And your first mission is to kill Sin." Lucifer said laying his hands on Murphy's shoulder. "Now awake."

. . .

"So gentlemen what is a United America. Between our three nations, by taking down our boarders we can increase productivity and inspire free trade, growing stronger economies. Our shared resources will decrease the price of manufacturing productivity, making us all a formidable force in the world trade. This could be bigger then the EU; with us at the helm as the four fathers of a new era." Langley spoke with such passion trying to convince the men. "Ask yourself; what good is it to either of our nations to continue with different currencies? One more valuable then the other, when we can support each other sharing in one currency bringing moe value to all of us." "And who will be at the center of all this?" "President Felex, what an excellent question my southern friend. As it already is, directed by God. Central America shall remain at the center." "And on what authority do you have to make this happen?" "President John Paul I was beginning to wonder if you were ever going to jump in. You see gentlemen, a Presidents reign or term I should say, last no more than eight years tops. But my position, and influence last a lifetime."

. . .

"I thought you were taking me to a ferry?" I asked as we reached a fishing dock in Uelen right on the edge of Chukotskiy Poluostrov. "Fishing boat, Ferry, it's all the same." The woman yelled through the window as she pulled off in a car. "Come now boy, it's time we be shipping off." A older heavy set man yelled, standing on the boat resembling a ship captain. I walked up the bridge connected to the ship, glancing over at the name written along the side. It read: The Leviathan. . . .

"Doo... Doo.." "Hello." Faith answered. "Hey." "Hey. Where are you calling from?" "This is my new number. i'm out in Los Angeles, and I thought maybe you wanted to get together." Murphy replied. "Well yeah, of course. Do you know where Santa Monica Pier is?" "Sure, I'll be there in half an hour." Murphy replied, while scrolling down on his laptop siphoning through all her recent emails and text. "Alright, I'll see you then." As the conversation ended they hung up the phone. Murphy continued to browse through her private emails, social media page, and text. Looking for anything that can give him a hint to where Love may be headed. He browsed through her photos looking for any link between Faith and Sin, but came up with nothing. He then closed the laptop tossing it into the passenger seat.As he started the honey gold Camero, giving the accelerator a tap causing the engine to roar, then pulled out into traffic.

. . .

The Leviathan sailed a lot smoother then one would imagine from a old ship. The captain came up deck standing in the door way as it opened. "It's best you get below now." He said stepping to the side with his arm extended out, gesturing for me to go down the stairs. "It's your ship." I said as I made my way in. The captain closed the door, sealing it as he twisted the lever. "Boooop.... Boooop." The red light flashed over head as the alarm sounded. "Is everything alright captain?" I asked preparing for an ambush. "All is well. We're beginning to submerge." He said nonchalantly "Submerge?" "Yes; like a submarine." The captain said brushing pass me leading the way. I had never seen, nor heard of such a ship like this. "You can bunk there." He said as we passed the barracks. "The dinning hall is down that way at the end. And down here is the engine room." He stated as we descended another set of steps. "How is everything running?" The captain asked one of his crew members. I began looking around as the two men conversed. I couldn't help but notice what looked like some sort of missile launch silo. "Excuse me captain, but what exactly are these?" I asked interrupting them. The captain turned around to see what I was referring to then replied. "You'll do best not to touch those. Don't even go near them." He said pointing to a sign as he walked passed me heading back upstairs. "This way." He continued as I stood there reading the sign that read: Nuclear War Heads. I followed the captain up through a second corridor that led to a large door. "This is the command room. Also the situation room, and my quarters. This ship is nuclear powered. It never has to leave the sea's if I don't want, and it's as armed as a battle ship. Indestructible and maybe the safest place in the world. So you go ahead and relax." He stated as he made himself comfortable. "Well that is the tour, you can find your own way back to your barracks right?" "Yes, I'll be fine." "Well good day sir." The captain finished then began to address his crew. I exited the room, and decided to get some rest. The distance was no more than a few hours, and once I get there, I don't plan on stopping until I'm back in California. . . .

"Hello Jinsu." The man said sitting in the seat behind him. "Hello Cain." He replied never turning around to face him. "Have you brought me any news of Loves where about?" "No sir, she seems to have dropped off the earth." "Well, we know thats impossible so why aren't you still out there looking?" "I hear another order has been set out for Celestial, if he has been sighted I would like to head the search." Cain was one of many hunters, ambitious and designated for search and destroy missions. He had once sat as a king of a nation, but was cursed to forever having to kill. "Cain, do you think that this will move you up in rank, because you believe one job is more important than that of another?" "No sir, I just haven't been able to fulfill my desire with a worthy battle for a long time." "Cain, Cain, Cain, ever bearing the mark I see. You just continue to do as you're told, and Russia will be yours to rebuild your kingdom." Jinsu stated never moving or looking back. "Yes sir." Cain replied as he got up to exit the church.

. . .

"Hey." Faith said smiling as she walked up on Murphy while he exit the car. "Hot dog on a stick?" She asked handing him one of the corndogs she held in her hands. "Thanks, so how you been?" He replied, taking the corndog as he leaned in to kiss her on the cheek. She smiled as she began to blush. "You're so forward Mr. Murphy." "Shall we?" He said lifting his arm for her to take a hold of it. The two began to walk the pier, stopping to enjoy the attractions as they conversed. After a few games, they decided to walk along the beach. The day had begun to die down as the sunset neared and People were beginning to leave. Leaving the sand empty, but for a few who remained. "So you came all this way alone?" "Well, yes and no. I have family who stay out here, so I'm not really alone." "So that's who you're staying with?" "No, I actually have a place of my own." "So soon?" Murphy questioned. "What about your place in Miami? And your cousin? What was his name? Sin; is that it?" Faith paused for a moment having been caught off guard by the question. Sin had been the reason that she was even there. He had left Faith with a house in Santa Monica, and the combination to a safe containing four hundred thousand dollars in cash. All so she would be able to start a new life. He had never planned to return to the house as it was just one of a few places he owned, that not even Love knew about. "It's ok, you don't need to answer if you don't want." Murphy stated. "No it's fine. I actually inherited the house, but now that I'm back I don't know how I ever left." She replied, avoiding talking about Sin. "How about you? Where are you staying?" "I don't know, I guess I hadn't given it much thought. I kind of came right over to see you, when I came into town." He stated looking for an offer. "Well it's getting late an kind of chilly. Maybe I should get some food in you, then take you home. Besides I need to find a place myself." "You don't have to do that. Theres more than enough room at my place." She replied. "I appreciate the offer, but I wouldn't want to intrude." "It's no problem, I promise." "Well if you insist, at least allow me to cook you dinner." He replied as he took her hand and led the way to the car.

. . .

"So gentlemen that concludes our business, and I promise you'll be all the better for having made your decision today." Langley said wrapping up the deal. Things were finally beginning to go exactly the way he wanted. "One question before we leave Langley." President John Paul stated. "Explain to me exactly why Central America, and not the United States?" "Because Central America is the linch pin that holds the America's connected." Langley replied then walked out of the room.

"Welcome to my home." Faith said as Murphy pulled into the drive way. Murphy couldn't help but admire the landscaping and colonial style mini mansion. "Feel free to look around. I'm just going to make myself more comfortable." She continued as she invited him into the house, then took her leave upstairs for a shower. Murphy walked through the house, turning on some music as he found his way to the kitchen. As he looked through the refrigerator he decided to go with something simple, but delicious. He pulled out a couple of steaks, a few sweet potatoes, rice and a onion. As the food was preparing he decided to thaw the vanilla ice-cream in the freezer sitting it on the counter. The yams were about ready as he began to prepare the plates. Laying the steak next to the side of rice, topping it with the caramelized onions. He opened a bottle of red wine, leaving it to ferment for a moment, as he took the yam's from the oven, scooping some on the plate. Just as he did Faith began walking in, wearing a silk thigh high night gown. Murphy was enthralled by the glow of her caramel colored skin, as it complimented the cream coloring of the gown. Her hair draped down to her breast, hanging outside of her face as to reveal her lip glossed lips. As his eye's continued to follow her legs back to her face. He realized, he had never really looked at her, not as he did in this moment. She was almost a completely different woman. He knew that she could be attractive under all her bruises when they had first met, but never like this. Such beauty combined with such a beautiful mind and spirit to create one gorgeous woman. "Can I help you?" She asked snapping him back to reality. "Sure, you can grab the wine." He said placing the pan back in the oven. She walked over and poured a glass, dancing to the music as she sung along with the lyrics. "Oh.. Excuse me." Murphy said, now standing face to face with her as she turned around nearly running into him. Murphy had never experienced anything quite like the way she was making him feel. He placed his hand along the side of her cheek, as he slowly moved in, placing his lips on hers. Faith welcomed his kiss as she gave into his embrace returning the kiss. With a sudden thrust Murphy lifted he off her feet sitting her on top of the counter. He ran his hands down her thighs, then lifted the gown above her waist. Revealing her bear skin as she wore no panties. He ran his hand across her moist vagina, then pressed her legs back. Murphy reached for the thawing ice cream, then dipped his fingers into the tub, scooping out a handful and rubbed it over her vagina. As the ice cream began to melt, dripping down her clitoris into the crevice, he began massaging her clitoris with his warm tongue. The cold from the ice cream mixed with the warm moister of his mouth, was enough to send her body into a confused shock of pleasure as she moaned, bitting down on her lip. This was something he had never done for any other woman, but something about her was different.

. . .

"Uuuu...Uhhh.." "Ahhh!" Sin yelled jumping out of his sleep in a cold sweat. This dream was something different from the others. A dream that didn't seem to be his own. The screams of a woman, and a young girl echo'ed through the air as he found himself on a old ship, drifting through a storm. The Mary Celeste was the name written along the side of the ship. Sin found himself trying to battle the storm, fighting the wind with only a sword and a pair of single shot muskets. Why would I be dreaming of a ship? Was there something about being aboard this ship that reminds me of something long forgotten? But how could that be, I have no memories beyond those form when I was born. Celeste, what was it about that name. "Knock, Knock!" "We're breaking surface Sir. Our ETA is ten minutes if you want to wait up on deck." "Thank you." I replied, then reached into my carry bag and grabbed the mouth wash. I took out a few loose bills, and put it in my pocket, then gathered my things and headed to the deck. Half a mile off the shores of Alaska, the captain ordered a U-boat to be released as a small door on the side of the ship opened like a garage door allowing a speed boat to pull out. "Over here sir." One of the crew men said, dropping a wooden ladder from the boat. I dropped my bag down to the man below, then climbed down the ladder into the boat. "Hang on to this." The driver said handing me a envelope and a set of car keys. I stood next to the driver as the boat splashed across the water, drawing closer to the shores. The icy breeze of the air seemed to cut my face as we pushed against the wind. The boat pulled along the shore of the beach as I prepared to exit. My boots splashed in the water as I jumped down. I grabbed my bag and walked over to a parked truck. Pushing the alarm button on the keys the doors unlocked as the truck started up. I threw my bag on the back seat as I got in, then opened the envelope to find a train ticket and a note that read: Fairbanks. I looked in the glove compartment then the arm rest in hopes of finding a map as I searched. I looked up noticing a folded paper sticking out of the visor. As I pulled the visor down, a map fell into my lap. I opened it in search for Fairbanks. Given it's distance plus the train ride, it would take me at least a couple of days to get to California. There had

Chapter 11

"Hello." Murphy answered awaking from his slumber. "Murphy, is this you? It's Langley." In all the time of his return Murphy had neglected to contact Langley. Something of an unusual occurrence. Had it simply slipped his mind given the time he's been spending with Faith, or was he now in a place to where he felt no need of answering to Langley. "Yes, it's me." "I'm glad to hear from you, but where the hell have you been?" Murphy gave it a moment, thinking of how to reply. Then answered, "I was going to contact you. I just needed some time to clear my head while I recovered." Recovered? What the hell happened to you?" "It's nothing Langley, I just needed some R&R." "Babe who are you talking to? It's 3:15 in the morning." Faith asked while rolling over in bed. "It's nothing. Go back to sleep." Murphy replied. "Murphy where are you? And who's with you?" Langley asked. "Listen, it's not a good time right now Langley, but I promise to contact you soon. I'll tell you everything when I get back. I have to go."

"Got damn it!" Langley yelled as the phone hung up. In his rage he threw the cell phone across the room. Murphy had turned over placing his arm around Faith, and went back to sleep; leaving Langley steaming in his own thoughts. "I swear, one day this job is going to kill you." A man dressed in a bath robe said as he poured two glasses of brandy. "Not now Jason." Langley replied as he took the drink. "I'm just saying you don't need the stress. Why don't you take some time off, and stay here in Texas with me?" Langley took a sip from his glass as he considered the offer. "There is just so much for me to do. I am on the verge of the biggest global economic merger ever produced, and now my most trusted asset is taking a hiatus when I need him the most." Langley stood up with his drink in hand, taking one large final gulp. Then ran his fingers through Jason's short cut blonde hair. "But maybe your right, come on let's get to bed." He said as he led the way to the room. Langley had only thought it was best to drop the subject. But what he wouldn't drop was his opportunity to unite, and reign over all the America's.

. . .

"Hello my dear, welcome home." The pope said extending his hand as Love kissed his ring. "What is it I can do for you?" He asked. "Where is sin?" "Not dead if that is what you're asking." Love's eyes widened as her heart dropped . "Then where is Aknubious?" "My dear Love always the ambitious one. You see my child there are consequences for every action, and to be the boss you must pay the cost. This time the cost has cost Aknubious." "My Lord please, you have to understand. My intent was never to undermine your reign, but only to extend mine while also furthering your progress of a one world government. Our loyalty was always to your throne." "So what is it you've come to ask of me today?" "Give me back Aknubious, and kill Sin/" "I see. But what is it you have to offer me in exchange for all this?" Love had found herself at a loss for words. What is it she really had to offer when he already had her soul, and anything else he wanted? "My Lord all I have to offer is my undying loyalty, and whatever else it is you may need." "Indeed." Lucifer replied, raising his hand as love suddenly became paralyzed. "What is Happening? what are you doing?" She screamed. "Relax my dear I'm about to nail that ass to the cross."

. . .

I finally arrived in Anchorage, and found myself eager to get to the airport. I once knew a man who was said to have moved out this way after retiring from the game. I once considered him a friend, but I'd hate for him to find me in town without first notifying him. Ghost would never believe I wasn't here to kill him. And then I'd probably have to kill him. Stealing souls had been on my mind a lot as of lately. That fight with Aknubious continued to push me beyond my limits. If I'm to survive it wouldn't hurt for me to increase my skills, maybe I'll make a stop at one of the local veterans hospitals. I was always one who respected the skills and knowledge of the past just as much as the advancements of the future. My mind had not yet sorted through all of Celestial's memories nor had my boy adjusted to his skills. Even still I was going to need some up to date talent. On my way to the airport I noticed a separate air strip with planes that read Fed-X along the side of them. This must have been their central office, and a convenient place for me to ship my things from. Once that was taken care of I was finally able to reach the airport, my flight wasn't due to leave for at least another hour. So I decided to take the time in between to catch up on some research as I was in front of a Cinnabon enjoying one of their cinnamon rolls. The Mary Celeste had continued to plague my mind as I searched through the web for any information regarding the name or ships, when I was finally able to stumble across picture of an old sailing vessel with the caption Ghost Ship written above it. I clicked on the icon for more information, and the story read:

In 1872 the Mary Celeste set sail for Genoa, Italy after loading it's cargo from New York. The ship was captained by a Mr. Al Celeste accompanied by a crew of eight men, and his wife, and daughter Mary Celeste. After several weeks at sea the Mary Celeste had not yet reached it's destination, on November 15th eight days after the Mary Celeste took sail a captain Moorehouse of the Dei Gratia set sails for Gibraltar. Three weeks later, Moorehouse sighted the Mary Celeste drifting at sea from what he described. The sails were up, but the ship was moving strangely through the water. As the Dei Gratia caught up with it, Moorehouse sent some men in a small boat to have a closer look. The men had all testified that everything on the ship had still been intact; the only thing missing was it's crew. Many of the men had said that none of the cargo was touched making it unlikely the ship had been attacked by pirates. But the strangest thing they said to be found was that the captain's belongings were still aboard and his daughter's toys layed on his bed, while all the while a meal was still cooking on the stove. The whole crew and all it's passengers simply vanished. No one knows what happened to them.

"Attention all passengers, due to the sudden change in the weather all flights are being grounded until further notice." The sudden eruption of frustration, and disappointed echoed through the airport. The airport personnel continued to inform the people of their options over the intercom. Advising those who preferred to stay in the airport to remain calm given the limited available space, and comfort ability, while also informing others on arrangements made with the nearby airport hotel. "For those who will like to stay in a room, all available rooms will be comp by the airport." There was no guarantee that many of us would even get a room, but neither of those options suited me. I had already sent my things ahead, and needed to be there when they landed. My only alternative was to catch a train into Canada, and hope to get a flight out, if not I'll have to get to Washington.

. . .

"Jinsu, where are we on Sin's where about's?" "The GPS on his phone currently puts him right outside of the Yukon territory. I would say he's right on track for arrival my Lord." "Has there been any new development on Celestials location?" "Not quite, but I have spoken with Cain. What is it you would have me do about the Love situation? There has been no development on her current location as well." "Do not bother yourself with Love; She is no longer a concern." "As you wish my Lord, and Sin?"

"I worried if Sin had ever managed to get back into Heaven he could pose a threat to my entire operation. But now that we know that want be a problem anymore. The value of his usefulness has become somewhat less than the risk of cleaning up behind him. Besides, there is no room for lukewarm." "I understand my Lord, and Murphy?" "See to it that Sin doesn't make it to California, and if he does keep Murphy on standby to finish the job." "Understood." Jinsu replied then hung the phone.

· · ·

"Love always the elusive one. No matter how hard I try, or how fast I run. I never seem to be able to catch you. So close yet so far, you escape my grasp like something I am never to have. In the day I am able to just come within a few feet of you, I will not hesitate, I will not blink, I will only put you sleep." Sin thought these words to himself as he watched the open planes pass by through the windows of the train. Knowing now that he and Love was somewhat of the same kind, the only thing that stood in his way now, was time. His heart was cold with vengeance, and no matter how long it took him, he would have his. And no one was going to stop him. Sin took this time to try and concentrate, focusing his mind on unlocking all that he had received from Celestial. Centuries of information pouring through his mind, images of times long forgotten. He began experiencing secrets of the world, secrets that would she the very existence of time, and history. So many lies, death, and distorted truth all for what. The fire burning deep within him begun to rise as his eye's and nose began to bleed. He could feel the flames ready to emerge from his eye's as his body dripped with sweat. "Sir, sir. Are you alright? Can you hear me? Sir!" Sin watched in a daze as his body slowly drifted to the floor. The mute sound of faces crowded around as they hovered over him. Darkness slowly closed in on the narrow hole of light as he watched the mute yelling faces faded into it.

Thou, thou, thou, thou, thou, thou. The sound of the choppers propellers echoed in my ears with a loud ringing. My eyes lazily opened as

I watched two men shouting over the roaring of the engine. As the ringing stopped I could hear them discussing on what to do with me. "Let's just drop him over the water, no one will find him." I knew then this wasn't a ride to a hospital. "Who is he?" "Does it matter?" "I guess not. You know you shouldn't even be here, I mean with you being a UFC champion in all. What if someone would have noticed you?" "Yeah, but when dutie calls you come running. I'd hate to have my contract cashed in early. Let's take him to the cabin, we can dispose of him there. Let the hell hounds feed on him." "Roger that." "I'll phone ahead, I haven't seen chaos since he trained me. And from what I remember he doesn't welcome unexpected guest very well." There was nothing I could do, my body was strapped down, and I couldn't move. Who was this Chaos? Was he another Jin? I knew something was wrong, those questions about Celestial were no more coincident, and now they want me dead. I knew the risk I was taking so there's nothing to regret now, if it's a war they want then it's a war they'll get. I continued to lay there playing asleep as I felt the chopper descending. The time table had just been pushed up, and the outcome was inevitable. I knew it would eventually come to this just not so soon. "Alright let's get him off." I could hear the sound of starving wolfs howling through the air. "Awww, look whose awake, dog food." "Ha, haha." The two men broke into a hysterical laugh as they hauled me from the aircraft. "Your a real bitch!" I shouted. The sudden outburst stunned the two having the desired effect. "Excuse me?" "You heard me. I see why you gave up your soul to be in the UFC, you were a bitch then, and you're a bitch now. If I wasn't tied to this shit I'd fuck you up." "You don't know me, you don't know shit about me!" He yelled dropping the gurney to the ground. "You think you know. I was cheated, robbed of my opportunity, because some drunken idiot decides to drive home. I lost everything, and did what anyone would have done. So yes I did whatever it takes, and now you sit here, and think you're better than me. You think you could beat me! Untie him!" "Scott come on let's just finish this." "No! Just shut the fuck up, and untie him." The pilot did as he was told, and released the restraints. As Scott began pacing back, and forth while he loosened the buttons on his sleeves then took his shirt off. As he did the pilot drew his knife, and backed away as I got to my feet. I raised my arms above my head and gave a good stretch, then reached for my toe's to stretch my legs. "You ready?" I asked. "I was born ready." He replied then broke into a sprint charging towards me. Still crouched over I grabbed a hand full of snow, and quickly threw it into his eyes, blinding him as I followed with a field goal kick to his nuts. I reached over picking up a broken tree branch as he fell to his knees holding his groin. "Maybe in the ring, but not out here." I gave one crushing swing bashing his head in, killing him instantly. "Ahhh! Son of a bitch." I dropped the tree branch as the pilot's knife lodged in my upper thigh. He immediately took off running as I yanked the knife out. "The coward." I thought as I grabbed Scott's body. Now here's one less soul they won't be getting. I knelt over the body and reaped it's soul. "Shit." Just as I did, I looked up then took off running as a pack of large wolf's came charging at me.

I ran weaving in between the tree's as they closed in. But no matter how hard I ran the snow seemed to fight against me. I would have to stand my ground; it was the only chance I had to survive before I was too tired to go on. With the knife clutched in my right hand, I spun around batting the first one out of the air, as I back handed it with my left. The second followed leaping into the air as I raised my arm lodging it into it's mouth to protect my throat. The force of the wolf's impact knocked me over causing us to fall back as I repeatedly thrust the knife into it's neck. As instant as I could roll over on top of it, I felt the sting of another one's teeth latch onto my right shoulder, and another on my left leg. Trying to prevent the first one from tearing off my shoulder, I bit down as hard as I could on the bridge of it's face, while jamming my left thumb into it's eye socket. The wolf gave out a loud cry as it's left eye finally burst, freeing me just long enough to turn over as I began to try and kick the other one off.It wasn't long before the first one was back at my throat again. At this rate they would surely rip me apart as one continued to drag me by the leg, and the other trying to pull me in the opposite direction. I continued to wrestle the first one away from my throat, slashing at it's face while simultaneously kicking the other in the nose. "Phrrrrrrrrrrrit! Pooooooow!" A loud whistle then the thundering exploding sound of a large rifle echoed through the air. The two wolfs scattered as the silhouette of a man appeared in the distance between the trees. I laid still tucking the knife, and my hand into the snow. "Get up Sin. We both know that I know you're not dead." The sound of a familiar voice caused my eyes to open. "Ghost?" "Hello Sin, long time no see." I quickly jumped to my feet, the sudden surprise although welcoming, baffled me, and yet the least of my problems. "How many guns do you have? There's bound to be more of those things out here, and at least two men." "Relax Sin, it's just us. I see you're still getting yourself into trouble. You're lucky they weren't hyenas." "What do you mean hyenas?" Instantly I realized, Ghost knew more about what was going on then I imagined. "What are you doing out here Ghost? I thought you were living somewhere in Alaska?" "Close enough right. Come now Sin you're smarter than this. It shouldn't take you this long to figure it out." "You're right, let's not play games. You're Chaos right? So let me ask, are you here to kill me?" "No Sin, whatever is going on I have nothing to do with it." "So then, where do you fit in all of this?" "My role has not yet to be played. Until the trumpet has sound, and my seal has been opened, my role is irrelevant." "You mean." "Yes. But I am not at liberty to say too much, nor do I know more than I'm supposed to. But I see you have embarked on a journey that has not yet shown where it leads. I feel this isn't the last time we will meet." "Then let me ask you one thing. The angels, where are they?" "Around, but Sin let me warn you. We all have a role to play in things even if we do not know what it is. The angels are not your friend; they have waged war against all of the fallen. They will not take kindly to seeing you." "Duly noted, now if you will I'd like to get back to that chopper. There are some things I need to take care of."

By the time Sin made it back to the cabin, he was already too late. The pilot had already taken off in the helicopter, leaving him now stranded in the wilderness. "Damn it; now how do I get out of here?" "You can always stay or I can take you." "Take me how? Do you have an invisible helicopter somewhere?" "No, but I can drive you to the coast where you can take a ferry into Seattle. From there I'm sure you can find your way to wherever you're going." "Well how long will that take?" "Does it really matter?" "It does, but if it's my only option, then I guess not." "My thoughts exactly. You should meet me around back, there's a blue pick up truck. Pull the tarp from over it, and you can wait inside. I'll be just a moment, I have to grab some things inside." I did as he asked and waited inside the cold truck, wondering if I should trust him. Just as I thought to get out of the truck, he emerged in the door way of the cabin. I shut the door as he walked over and got in. "Here you may need this." He said reaching under his shirt. I quickly leaned over and grabbed his wrist as the butt of a gun was revealed. "Easy Sin; take it, it's for you." I pulled the gun from his waist and returned back to my seated position. I examined the gun as he started the truck and allowed the engine to heat up. I ran my fingers across the engraving that read. (Destruction) I then pulled my phone out and rolled down the window, tossing it out into the snow I fired one loud thundering shot that echoed through the forest causing the phone to shatter into little pieces. "Good thinking." He said smiling as he backed the truck out. The gun was truly amazing, a custom work of art I had never seen before. It's accuracy was unbelievable and the recoil was as smooth as a summers breeze. I smiled giving only one thought to myself. Chaos and Destruction.

. . .

"Sir my apologies, he got away and Scott's dead." The pilot yelled into the phone as he flew across the pacific. "I understand, you will not be punished for your incompetence. Return to New Orleans immediately, we have to take a trip." "Yes Sir, I'm on my way." Jinsu hung p the phone and called for his driver. "Yes boss." The man said as he entered the room. Jinsu reclined back in his chair and touched his finger tips together in the shape of a pyramid. "Boyd, I think it's time we take a trip. Pack up everything of importance and prepare to leave. Keep in mind we ant be returning." "Yes sir, right away."

. . .

As Love laid there on the floor, her body unclothed against the cold stones of the Pope's chambers, she for a moment considered her life, and what has become of it. She rubbed her hand across her stomach as she could feel an unholy and unnatural child growing inside of her. And for the first time in a long time, she wept. A silent cry of tears covered the floor as they ran down her face. The light from the doorway shined upon her skin as Lucifer opened the door. Grabbing his robe off a hook to clothe his naked body as he left the room. The light slowly drained from the room as the door closed. Leaving Love to remain in the darkness, holding her stomach as her tears turned into puddles.

. . .

Once I had finally made it to Seattle, my challenge had just begun. How was I to get home? Me making it there before my things was no longer an option. And with them hunting for me, using the only I.D I had with me would put me smack dead on the radar. In my pocket was no more than a thousand dollars, less than that, because the ferry had just cost me two hundred dollars. Now I would need a cab, and there's no telling how far I may need to go. I just hope I'll have enough for a train ticket, and that's at least a two day ride.

. . .

Ring…Ri..ng. "Hello." "You're up, Sin may be headed in your direction, So I'm going to need you to keep an eye out. (So I'm going to need you to keep an eye out.) Unfortunately we've lost track of him." "This is a big city, if you can't locate him, how do you expect me to?' "Have faith. I've also alerted the local authorities, so you'll have help. End this before he becomes a problem." "I got it." "Good." Lucifer hung up the phone then turned around in his chair, placing his feet on the desk in front of him. "Bring him in." He said to the guard standing at the door. As it opened he waved his hand in a gesture to come in. "Hello brother." "Hello Jinsu, it's been a long time sense we've been in the same room together. Have a seat, and tell me, to what do I owe the pleasure of you being here?" "It's Sin, we need to talk about Sin."

Chapter 12

"Please prepare for departure, we are now approaching our final destination. Last stop Los Angeles Union Station." I took in a deep breath and held it for a moment then released. It was good to be back home. With only $200 dollars on hand, I would have to spend it wisely. Good thing I had a condo right here in downtown. So I wouldn't have to go far. The doors opened and the sound of the downtown city streets came to life. A smile came over my face as I stepped onto the platform. I took in another deep breath then thought to myself, I was finally home. As I exited the platform and walked through Union Station a sense of uneasiness came over me as if I was being watched. Every security guard I passed seemed to avoid direct eye contact with me, as they watched me from their peripheral vision while talking into their radios. Im just a few steps from the door, if I can just make it outside I'm free. As I pressed the door open the heat from the sun rays shined. It burned me as the light became blinding to my eyes. With both eyes squinted I walked through the traffic then out through the parking lot. As I reached the side walk I glanced over my shoulder and noticed two patrol officers cutting across the parking lot on foot. With no time for hesitation I stepped out into the street weaving through traffic. Once across I cut across the open square heading for 4th and Temple. Even if I could make it to Hill or Grant I could use the metro station to loose the trail. As I walked through the square I noticed a police car pulling up on the street ahead. "Damn it." I doubled back and noticed the two officers on foot coming in on the other side. They were attempting to box me in. I noticed a large crowd and immediately joined in. I purchased a hat from one of the street vendors then took off my jacket throwing it in the trash as I blended in with the crowd. I then took a seat behind a pair of musicians and watched as the police came together and decided on which way to look. After a moment I stood up and bought a hot dog from one of the stands then proceeded to walk out with the crowd. As we reached the street, I waited for a on coming bus to make it's stop. I had to get off the streets. "Aye don't I know you?" "Excuse me." "Yeah you. Where you from." "Listen not now." As this strange man persisted to challenge me to an altercation, my only concern was to not draw attention and to get on the bus. In that instant I began to experience a new heightened sense of awareness, as my right hand reached for Destruction and I noticed in my peripheral vision the arm of a Police officer extending over the crowd. As the doors to the bus opened I heard the officer yell. "Freeeeze!" Followed by the two burst of gun fire. "Boom! Boom!" I ducked then ran onto the bus catching one in the shoulder as I shielded the driver. "Boy get off me!" "Bitch drive!" I yelled drawing Destruction from my waist. As the bus began to move I watched through the glass of the door as two officers gave chase, shooting at the tires. The bus swerved and crashed onto the curb as it came to a stop. I jumped from the floor and pulled the lever to open the door then grabbed the driver as I ran out. I could kill them, two thunders roars from destruction would cause mass panic, but with everyone watching they'ed be able to explain why they opened fire on me in public. And if I'm going to hide, I'll need the public on my side. We ran out of the front door and around the front end of the bus as bullets zipped by. "Please just let me go." "Keep running!" I yelled as I held tight to her arm dragging her along. True enough I could be moving faster without her, but for all those camera's watching I'm not the only one they're shooting at. We ran across the street turning a left on Hill. "Come on we can loose them down here." "Boy I'm not trying to loose them, let me go." We ran into the subway station, there were trains coming in and some already going out. I continued to lead her down to the lower level as I could hear the arrival of the next train. Right behind us was at least a dozen officers, and screams for help made it easier for them to follow. Without her noticing, I took the badge and wallet from her pocket. As we reached the train I let her go and ran ahead to catch the doors before they closed, then immediately ran to the back of the train using the drivers exit, and hid in the shadows of the tunnel as the train pulled off. The officers ran to the train yelling for it stop, but it was already going. "Come on, radio ahead we can catch him at the next stop." To the bus drivers surprise their concern for her was none. The officers had paid her no attention as they continued on with their pursuit. I watched the woman as she took out her phone, and proceeded to call someone. I opened the wallet and read the name on the I.d badge. Ethereal Branton. As I climbed out of the rail way, she continued to talk into the phone to what sounded like her boss as I approached from behind. "Alright, alright, I'm on my way back. Stupid ass Bitch." She said after hanging up the phone. "I need your help." The sudden surprise of my voice scared her as she jumped and spun around. "Oh hell nah." She said as she tried to take off running. "Wait!" I yelled slamming her against the wall. "Get off of me." "Listen." "No; get you're damn hands off me." "I need your help." "You know what, they don't call me Tia for nothing." "And what does that suppose to mean?" "Tough, Intelligent, and attractive." And with that said she stomped on my toe's and followed with a left hook across my eye, then a knee to my groin. As I went down she attempted to run. I grabbed her ankle tripping her to the floor then drew my gun. "You do that again I'll shot you. Now get up and call for someone to come get you." "My boyfriend won't like this shit at all." "And I'm sure he wouldn't like to get his ass kicked or shot in the ass even more. Now get him on the phone."

. . .

"Are you watching the news?" "Yes of course." "Then tell me what type of bullshit have you created?" "My Lord forgive me. My men were more afraid of what may happen if they lost him…" "Save it, because they lost him anyway. I'll deal with this." Lucifer hung up the phone crushing it in his hand. "Jinsu! Get Langley on the line, have him pull any past information that even looks like it pertains to Sin. And when he has something, forward it to Murphy."

. . .

"You know your not looking to good." "Just keep walking." "I'm serious, you may need a doctor." "Where is your boyfriend?" She was right, my shoulder had managed to heal, but the bullet was still lodged in there. It was starting to cause poor blood circulation, and my arm was beginning to go numb. "Here he is." "Alright, open my door then get in." "Babe what the fuck is this?" "Look it's a long story just…" "Just drive." I said jumping in the back seat showing him the gun. "Look man we don't…" "Look nothing, just take me to 1050 South Grand Avenue." "Babe, what the fuck have you got me into?" "Me; I called you because I needed your help. But I see now that was a bad idea." "Please, the both of you stop talking. And you, just drive." "Look you ain't no kinky ass rapist are you?" "You're really full of yourself aren't you? No I'm not. As long as you help me I promise you'll be alright." I admit her hazel brown eyes and yellow skin made for a gorgeous woman, but I was no monster.

. . .

"Hello." "Murphy Sin's in town, we're running through all past records and associates. The police are checking into them, stay on alert." "How do you know he's in town?" "He was spotted getting off the train." "Then what?" "Local police tried to take him, it was a big incident. He kidnapped a bus driver and more." "Where is that bus driver now?" "I don't know." "Cancel all other searches, he's too smart to go somewhere you may look. Focus on that driver, find out who it is, and track their phone." "Right away." "Hey what's going on?" Faith asked walking out of the gas station. "Nothing, just work. You ready?" "Yeah we can go."

. . .

"Why don't you go by Ethereal? It's a beautiful name. What does it mean?" "It means, extremely delicate and light in a way that seems too perfect for this world, Intangible. How do you know my name?" I tossed the wallet into her lap. "So your a thief to?" "I never stole anything, it's all there." "If you don't mind me asking, who are you?" "My name is Anoku, well my real name is Annunaki. It means the powerful one, but people call me Sin." "What did you do? Why were the police trying to kill you?" "That's a whole other story, if I told you, you wouldn't believe me." "So now I guess you want to go on a date with him to?" "Don't even start, here you go with that bullshit." "Hey!" The sudden burst of my elevated tone sent a shock wave through the car. "Don't start this again." "You're not looking to good, you're getting worst." "It's fine we're here now. Pull over right there." "So I guess you'll let us go now?" "Not yet." "But why? We did as you asked." "I just need help getting up stairs." "I thought you said you were fine?" "Well I'm not!" My body had begun to breakout in a sweat. I assumed the led from the bullet had entered my blood stream, and I needed to get it out before it killed me. "So what do you want now?" "Help me out of the car, then help me get up stairs and you're free to go." "Fine." I could see her frustration as she flung the door open and got out. "Come on. And you could get out and help me." She said to her boyfriend as she opened my door. Just as I had one foot out of the car. "Sceeeert!" The tires screeched as the car pulled off, causing me to fall on top of her. "Oow!" I can't believe this. You... Ooow!" I stood up and helped her from the ground. "Move, I don't need your help, I got it." The sudden betrayal and abandonment had shattered her heart, and infuriated her. A feeling I knew all to well. "Let's just get you inside, so I can be on my way."

. . .

"Sir I think we got something." "What is it?" "Our bus driver is a Ms. Ethereal Branton. We've been tracking her phone, and it seems she's stopped for a great deal of time in this area here. We ran the address against any known places of residence on a Mr. Anoku and we've got a hit. This same location she's been at for over thirty minutes, he also owns a condo there." "It's as good a shot as any, Good work." Ring... Ring... "Go ahead Langley." "Jinsu we may have something. We found the driver, she's at a downtown condominium. The address is 1050 South Grand Avenue, Sin also owns a condo there." "Good work, keep an eye out, but do not engage him." "Yes sir."

Ring... Ring. "Yeah." "Murphy I'm sending you and address. I need you to check it out, immediately." "Will do." Murphy hung up the phone and turned the car around. "Where are you going?" "I just need to check on something for work. It shouldn't take long." "Is everything alright?" Faith asked with a worried look on her face. "Everything's fine, even better I should say."

. . .

"Look I got you home right? Now you're just asking for too much." "Listen, I just need you to stab me right here, then place the other knife in next to that one and pull them apart. Just hold it open long enough for my muscles to push the bullet out. It's not like you haven't been wanting to. Trust me I'll make it worth your wild." "I don't want nothing from you, I just want to go." "Fine, grab that black bag over there, both of them." "Here now can I go?" "Yeah, take that bag with you and grab those keys over there." I unzipped the other bag and pulled out a .45 caliber colt 1911 with a suppressor attached to the front. "What are you doing?" "It doesn't concern you. There's five hundred thousand dollars in that bag, and those keys are to a black Range Rover sitting in the parking lot. Stall one fifty seven. You can go whenever you're ready." I put the muzzle of the suppressor to my shoulder right where the bullet should be. I could have just cut it out through the front, but I was pressed for time and needed to keep moving. "Wait; I'll help you." "No need." Fap! A single shot ripped through my shoulder and out the back, dragging everything with it as a large hole opened up. I flew off the stool hitting my head on the floor and fell unconscious. Ethereal began to panic as she watched Sin's body lay motionless on the floor. Her first reaction was to head for the door, as she grabbed the keys and reached for the door handle. For a slight moment she began to feel empathy for him, releasing the door knob as she turned around, and returned to his body. To her surprise he was still breathing. She contemplated calling an ambulance, but was afraid of what the police might do. She was stuck in a situation and had no idea of what to do. She grabbed a towel from the kitchen thinking she could at least try to stop the bleeding by putting pressure on the wound. When she noticed the strangest thing she had ever seen. His shoulder was beginning to repair it's self. She dropped the towel in disbelief as she stood up and backed away from him. She couldn't believe what her eye's were seeing, if they were really seeing it at all. She grabbed the keys once more, this time taking the bag with her as she headed for the door. She thought to herself as she ran down the hall. "Am I loosing my mind? That couldn't have been real." As she made it to the parking lot she continued to press the alarm button looking for stall one fifty seven till she found it. Once she sat in the car she took a moment to try and compose herself. As she gripped the steering wheel to stop her hands from shaking, then took a deep breath. Once she had calmed down and collected herself, she started the car and pulled out. As she was exiting the parking structure, she passed the car of a young woman, and man that was coming in. An ire feeling had come over her as they locked eye's while the two cars passed. This came as no concern to her. She had done her part, and was free to go, but why then did she feel the need to go back? Why had she pulled over to even give it a second thought?

. . .

him no choice. He knelt down and did as he said, rising slowly leaving the gun hanging to his side. "Now what?" "Draw it." "No; you already have the drop on me." Murphy began to slowly lower his weapon, as Sin walked over to a window and stare out of it. "It's no use thinking about running. There's nothing for you out there. The place is surrounded by cop's who will gun you down the moment you walk out on that street." "I should warn you Murphy. It won't be easy to kill me, I'm not the same as I was." "Nor am I. Now stop stalling, I know you're wondering about the girl, but don't, she's already gone." "Well it's just me and you then?" "We knew it would come to this some day." "Yeah." Sin spun around dashing across the room as Murphy opened fire. both men exchanged shots that nearly took the others head off. "Click! Click!" Both guns had locked and ran empty as both men slid across the floor ducking for cover. "You out?" "I got one more clip, You?" Sin thought about Destruction, but he knew the heightened senses it gave him would surely be the end of Murphy. But what was he to do? "Im out, my last magazine is in there with you." He yelled form the other room. "I guess that means I win then right?" "If that's how you want to win." Sin replied clutching the handle of destruction, trying to fight the urge it gave him. Murphy peeked around the couch, and noticed that Sin wasn't lying there waiting to ambush him. "Where is it?" "Where is what?" "Your magazine?" "It's in the black duffle bag." Murphy dragged the bag behind the couch and looked inside. What he found was one magazine, a pair of identity's and a large amount of cash. "You planning on going somewhere?" "Yeah; to hell." Murphy smiled at the reply, then zipped the bag and slid it across the floor into the room. "I tell you what Murphy, if you beat me you deserve to walk out of here." "I'll keep that in mind." Both men reloaded there weapon then prepared for the final dual. "You ready?" "Ready." Sin appeared from around the corner as Murphy leaped from behind the couch. "Pow! Pow!" Two shots from a snipers riffle broke through a window knocking Sin to the ground. Murphy had been cheated and robbed of his glory. He spun around and opened fire on the roof top across the way. Sin had gotten back to his feet and grabbed his bag. Murphy turned around to check on Sin and noticed he was gone. When he suddenly heard the sound of a window break in the other room. After Sin grabbed his bag he fired a few rounds through a window as he ran and jumped through the glass onto the fire escape. Murphy ran to the window but was too late. Sin had jumped down a construction shoot and slid down onto the parking structure. "Damn it!" Murphy then turned around and ran back to the elevator.

As Sin reached the parking structure he quickly got to his feet then ran down into the stairwell. He leaped staircase to staircase as he rushed to the bottom then crashed through the door. The sudden loud screeching of a door opening, followed by the loud slamming of it closing echo'ed through the parking lot, causing Faith to jump in her seat, as her attention was caught by a man running across the lot. "Sin?" She said to herself just as the elevator doors were opening up. "Phap! Phap!" Click. Murphy fired two shots missing before the gun went empty. "Damn it!" Murphy jumped in the car and grabbed the gun from the glove compartment, then started the car and sped off. "What is going on?" Faith screamed. "Nothing just sit back."

Sin had made it down to the car's entrance and noticed the police car's waiting outside. He swung the bag over his shoulder, holding the 1911 in his left hand and destruction in his right. He took a deep breath and let his mind begin to focus then in a great irruption ran out. The thunderous roar of destruction caused everyone to panic as they all took cover. One shot through the gas tank of one of the squad cars and a chain reaction of exploding cars erupted. The more destruction he caused the redder his eye's became, as if they were filling with blood. Ethereal pulled her head from the steering wheel as she heard the explosion and watched as people ran pass creaming. She looked in the rearview mirror and witnessed Sin running and ducking as the 1911 continued to flash, knocking officers to the ground.

The sound of screeching tires echo'ed out of the parking structure catching Sin's attention as the headlights of a car and it's roaring engine drew closer. As the car shot out of the exit, drifting on it's tires. Sin spun around raising Destruction now fully immersed in it's power and pointed at the driver. An in an instant time seemed to have stood still. The sight of the gun locked on Murphy, but his eye's were locked on Faiths. Sin lowered Destruction then spun around and took off running.

"No, no no, no. Please don't come this way." Ethereal said to herself watching Sin run in her direction. She started the car an begun to pull off. "Tia!" Sin continued to yell as he sprinted to catch the truck before Murphy ran him down. He grabbed a hold of the rear railing on top of the truck then jumped on the rear bumper. Sin swung the gun and knocked out the back window then climbed in. Just as he did Murphy's car slammed into the rear bumper.Sin took the 1911 and fired into the hood of Murphy's car trying to shut the engine down. Murphy began to swerve side to side then sped up, trying to pull along side the truck. "You have to drive faster, floor it!" Sin yelled. As Murphy pulled along the side of them, Ethereal slammed on the breaks causing him to shoot pass as she made a hard right turn. "Woo! That's what I'm talking about." Ethereal began to smile as Sin cheered her on. "Don't stop now Tia, we're not clear yet." Sin looked over ahead and watched as a police helicopter closed in on them. Ethereal continued to keep her speed up, drifting in and out of traffic. "Where are we going?" "Just keep driving, and head for the freeway."

"Kyle stop. Just let him go." "I can't, you wouldn't understand." "What wouldn't I understand?" "Not now Faith, hang on." Murphy made a sharp turn hook sliding around the corner. "Alright, there they go."

"Looks like we got company, get on up here." "Oh my God, why are you doing this to me? How did I get mixed up in this?" Ethereal said to herself as she pulled onto the freeway. Sin watched as Murphy and a dozen squad cars followed. He looked up to the helicopter hovering above them then raised destruction. Four thundering roars and the helicopter came crashing down on the squad cars.

"Holy shit!" Murphy yelled as he swerved out of the way the of debrie. "You see; he's lost his damn mind." Faith gave no reply to him, she continued to remain quiet in her seat.

"This is becoming far to much for me. I don't want to do this." Ethereal yelled to Sin. "Listen, as soon as I can get you out I will, but right now focus on driving." Sin heightened senses started to kick in as he was drawn to look to his left, where he noticed Murphy's car coming around a conjoining on ramp. "You gotta move it Tia."

"I know your mad, but I promise this will be over soon." Murphy said as they pulled onto the freeway behind Sin. He pointed his gun out of the window and took aim. "The freeway splits up ahead, which way should I go?" Ethereal yelled. "Go left!" Sin replied as he watched Murphy try and lock on to him.

"Kyle you should stop." "Don't worry; it's almost over." "I know." With that said Faith grabbed the steering wheel, yanking it to the side as they ran into the devider. The car flipped becoming airborne as Sin yelled for Ethereal to stop the car. Cars all around slammed on their breaks as the car continued to flip, bouncing off the ground, before sliding on it's roof until it came to a stop. "Sin; where are you going?" "Just go. Get out now." He ordered as he got out of the truck. Sin ran down to Murphy's car and drew destruction. As he came around the car he found Murphy cradling Faith's body as he grieved over her. Seeing Sin's shadow he reached for his gun. "Don't; you'll never make it." "What do I care?" "I can save her. The same way I tried to save you." "Then do it!" Sin lowered his gun then knelt down next to the body, then placed his hand on her chest. As he did a strange sudden occurrence of rain began dropper down. As usual his arms began to glow, but this feeling he got was different, it reminded him of Celestial. As he continued his entire body began to light up, then in an instant everything became clear to him.

As Faith eye's opened she immediately looked to Sin. "What have you done? You have to go Annunaki." "He's not going anywhere." Murphy said lifting his gun. "Kyle please." "I have to Faith!" "If you kill me Murphy, she go's to hell with me." "You lie." As we spoke, lighting and thunder began to cover the sky, then a man's voice spoke from behind me. "No he's not." "And who are you? You got nothing to do with this." "On the contrary, Annunaki has something in his possession that doesn't belong to him, and I want it back." "I don't know you, and I don't have anything of yours." Sin replied. "Of course you do, that angel soul. Give it to me!" Sin raised destruction and pointed at the mans face. "The way I see it, that soul is my only bargaining chip. So if you want it, take it." And in a blinding movement the man grabbed Sin's arm striking him in the face with a reverse elbow. Dis arming him as he shoved him up against the car. "You think a few angel souls give you the power to defeat me? Don't you know who I am Annunaki?" "Seraph No!" "Quiet Faith! You've made enough of a mess already. You should have turned him over the minute you found him." "Let him go." Murphy said now holding destruction. "That's some power kid. You sure you can handle it?" "You sure you want to find out?" Seraph then grabbed Sin by the throat and began to squeeze. "You kill me, and that precious angel soul go's back to the dungeon with me." Seraph thought for a moment then released Sin, fixing his suit as to regain composure. "Well then, I guess we can call this a stalemate, but this is far from finished." And just as fast as lighting struck again, Seraph was gone. "I think that belongs to me?" Sin told Murphy. "Who was that guy?" "He's Seraph the most highest of the angels." "What did he want from you?" "Her." Murphy looked to Faith who had no words. "She is the angel of Faith and Hope." Sin answered as he took destruction from Murphy. "The way I see things is you owe me." "What do you need?" "Right now I need to know where Langley is, and I need to get out of here."

Chapter 13

"Come on!" Ethereal yelled as the black Range Rover pulled up. "I thought you wanted out?" "Come on, we don't have time for this." "Stick with her Murphy, I'll contact you." I ran and jumped in the passenger seat of the truck as Ethereal pulled away from the scene of the accident. Murphy had given me Langley's location. He owned a ranch, said to be on the edge of El Paso, Texas. If I was to sneak up on the head of the snake, I would have to come from behind, and climb the body. But I couldn't drag Ethereal into this any further. "Listen; thanks for coming back, but we need to split up, and lose this car." "Alright, if you think so. What do we do?" "Get off here, there should be a Greyhound station a couple blocks over. Pull into that private parking lot, we'll leave the car there, and call you a cab." "What about you?" "It's better you don't know, for both our safety." "If you think so." I couldn't afford to be stranded on a bus with here knowing where I was going. I had to disappear again, and I couldn't leave traces or trails to follow.

. . .

"Jinsu; what in the hell is going on? He's become more trouble now than he's ever been. How hard is it to kill one man?" "My Lord maybe it's time to reconsider your up coming tour. Just until this is over with." "Are you suggesting that I hide, because Sin is running loose out there." "No my Lord, I would never suggest that. All that I am saying is we should get a handle on the situation before we focus on parading you around to the public." "No; we continue on with the schedule, it's important that the people see their king sometimes. It reminds them to love him, and no town bit Annunaki will come between that. Find him!" "Understood."

. . .

After reaching the Greyhound station, I boarded a bus headed for El Paso. Faith's new found soul provided me with more clarity and strength to go on. So much information, it was as if I remembered everything. It's power even made it easier for me to adapt with Celestial's. I felt I was ready to fully unleash it's power and memories. I believe now I'm ready to handle it, and for what I had planned I would need it. With a long ride ahead of me, I think I'll take this time to meditate on doing just that.

"What's the matter Langley?" "Jason I can't help but think, maybe you were right. I should have took a break while I had the chance. Now I couldn't want to be there with you anymore." "You can always come back." "No; not this time. I have to be here." "Well you know best Langley. But you know I'll be here when you're ready." "I know Jason, I love you." "I love you to, I'll talk to you later." "Alright." Langley hung up the phone rubbing his hand across his neck. The stress of the day was beginning to get to him. He was now tasked with the burden of finding Sin, and making the current event's in Los Angeles look like a terrorist attack. This isn't what he envisioned, not here, not now.

Sixteen hours later I was arriving in El Paso. As my eye's opened everything had become so clear to me now. The bus had come to it's final stop. I grabbed my bag and fined the line to exit the bus. El Paso was a hot and dry place. The humidity alone caused my body to sweat. It reminded me of an old style, at any minute I expected a cowboy to walk out, like in an old western. I walked over to a small stand where a man was selling old style cocoa cola, and pepsi bottles of soda, along with carne asada tacos. I purchased a soda and two tacos. When the man gave me my change, I asked that it be in all coins, then walked to the pay phone. Doo... Doo...

fence and grabbed the bag as I ran across the lawn. I stopped along the side of the house and gave it a moment, but still no ambush. I worked my way around to the back door, and checked the handle. It was unlocked. This was just way to easy. I thought for sure the party must have been waiting inside. I pulled out destruction and slung the door open as I ran in. To my surprise there was no one here. I searched through the entire house, but there was no one. Murphy had burned me, so I thought as I searched the upstairs bedroom. Until I noticed a pair of headlights coming up the drive way as I looked out of the window. As the car pulled into the garage I ran downstairs and waited. I could hear the car door as I made it to the garage door. As soon as the door opened, "Wam!" I punched the man directly in the nose then drew destruction, surveying the room as the man fell to the ground. Once I realized he was alone, I turned my attention back to the man, who's nose was now bleeding, and began to ask questions. "where is Langley?" "I think you my nose." "Where is Langley!" I asked again kicking the man in his ribs. "I don't know! Who are you?" I grabbed the man by his hair and drug him into the house. "Get up!" I yelled pulling the man from the ground then pressed the barrel of the gun under his chin. "I'm going to ask you one last time. Where is Langley?" "I don't know who you're talking about." "You don't, do you?" "No, Ahhh!" A solid left hook across his chin knocked him back to the floor. "Then who the hell is this!?" I yelled grabbing a picture of him and Langley off the wall, then slapped him in the face with it. "Get him on the phone if you want to live." "You do it!" He yelled, tossing his cell phone to my feet. Ring... Ring... "Hey, you made it home?.. Jason.. Are you there?" "How are you Langley?" "Who is this?" Langley asked snapping his fingers for his assistant to come. "Don't play dumb Langley, you know exactly who this is. And don't bother calling for any help over here. If I see anybody he's dead." "What do you want Sin? He has nothing to do with this." "Get up." Sin ordered as he escorted Jason into the kitchen. "Now sit down, and take off your clothes." "What are you doing Sin?" "Don't worry Langley, I'm not going to ravage your sweet little as candy. What I want is Lucifer." Sin replied placing a large ladle spoon on the eye of the stove, then grabbed an oven glove. "Sin, I can't give you that. I don't have that kind of power." "Langley, in another minute this ladle will be as red hot as a branding iron. If you don't give me what I want in the next minute, I'm going to scoop his precious little into this burning hot ladle. Do you understand?" "Got damn it Sin! Alright, what exactly do you want?" "Tell me when, and where he's going to be."

Doo… Doo… "Hello." "Murphy it's me, I got him. Now I need you to do me a favor. Contact this number, you ready?" "Go ahead." "451-751-902-20 the mans name is Celestial. Tell him everything that I'm about to tell you. It's happening now, and we have to act soon."

Sin explained the details of his plan to Murphy as he walked through Langley's house pouring flammable cleanser on everything including the electrical sockets. "Come on; you're coming with me." He said to a now hog tied Jason, as he carried him to the trunk of the car. He struck a match and tossed it into the house, then got in the car an drove off.

"Ring..Ring." "What is it Langley?" "Sir, it's about Sin." "what is it?" "I think Murphy has been compromised. Sin managed to corner me, at a private estate i owned. There were only three people who knew where it was, and some how Sin found it." "where is Sin now?" "I don't know, but I know where he's going to be. He forced me to tell him when and where you will be upon arrival. I think he's going to attempt to assassinate you. I think we should cancel the tour, and use a decoy to trap him." "No; we will continue on, and use this to ur advantage. He'll never come close to me, he'll attempt to do it from a far." "And Murphy?" "Place Murphy at my side with my detail. We'll see where his loyalty lie's." "As you wish my Lord."

Doo…Doo. "Hello." "Is this Celestial?" "Who's calling?" "My name is Murphy, Sin told me to contact you." "Regarding what?" "He needs you. Theres a plane ticket waiting at the airport for you, under the name Vic Kelly. I'll be waiting when you land. We have much to talk about." "I'm on my way."

"Jinsu, I've just heard the most wonderful news. Our dear Annuaki seeks to cut the head off the serpent. how wonderful is this?" "Shall I top the security at the airport?" "No, look for the most unusual, but effective snipers perch. That's where he will be, but don't move on him until after he takes his shot. The Holy Arch Bishop assignation attempt that failed do to divine interference from God. What better way to solidify the divine power of a Pope, from here on. This will forever be in their hearts and minds. Prepare the jet Jinsu, it's time we leave." "Yes Sir."

Doo, Doo.. "Hello." "B.B it's me." "Annoku? Man where have you been? I thought I seen you on the news downtown yesterday." "it's a long story, but I need your help." "Anything, name it." "You remember the time I went to Cube?" "Yeash, how could I forget, some of our finest work." "Well, I need to do it again. This time better." "Not a problem bro, stop by anytime." "See you soon."

"So you're going through this?" "I have to. If he's going to put his life in danger that's fine, but I won't loose you because of it." Ring..Ring. "Go ahead." "Murphy it's Langley?" "I have a job for you." "Is there someone else you can out on this assignment?" "No; its priority one. I need my best guys on it." "What is the mission?" "The Pope is flying in Tomorrow to start his annual parade around the nation. They've requested our top guys to assist with the security detail. I'm placing you right at his side the moment he exit's the plane." "What time will this be?" "Approximately thirteen hundred hours. So i need you present by nine a.m for final rounds of inspection." "Where at?" "Ontario airport. The parade will cross through Pasadena, then return. From there you'll fly with him to D.C as he attends the White House." "Will do. Will you be there." "No, but I'll be in D.c when you get there." "See you then." "Till then." Murphy hung up the phone and let out a deep breath. "What is it?" "It's nothing, I just hate to get you involved in all of this." "What do you mean?" "I've been called to secure the Pope's arrival tomorrow. It's also when I was to meet Celestial. I may need you to pick him up. All you have to do is give him this bag, and

I'll right down everything Sin wants him to know." "No need." Murphy spun around drawing his gun as a voice spoke out behind him. "Who are you? And what do you want?" "I'm Celestial. Hello Faith." "Faith do you know him?" "Yes. He is who he say he is." "But how are you here?" "I was expecting your call, so I traced it when you did. When you had called I was already on my way here. You just provided me with an address for when I landed." "Why didn't you just tell me?" "I had to know I could trust you, But what I didn't expect is her." Murphy lowered the gun and sat it on the dresser. "I guess that solves that problem then." "Indeed. now you mentioned having a bag for me." "Yeah, it's right there." Celestial opened the bag to find a snipers riffle, an MK5, two suppressors, and a stick of C-4. "I guess we do have a lot to talk about. We better not waste time."

"Jinsu, where is the Leviathan?" "To my knowledge it should be docked in Miami." "Good; when Sin makes his move, I want you to see to it that his body is dragged through the gates as well." "Will do Sir." "Tell me; where do you think he will strike?" "Let's just hope it's not while we're up in this plane."

Chapter 14

"Good morning, did you stay awake all night?" Murphy asked noticing Faith sitting at the edge of the bed as he awoke. "Aren't you even a little bit worried? Do you not find it odd that the day the Pope is in town, Sin is also planning something huge?" "What are you saying?" "I don't know, I'm just worried about you?" "Why? I have nothing to do with it." "I've seen this many times before and it never ends well. When men get like this, they'll stop at nothing destroying anything, and anyone in their way." "I'm more worried for you, than my own sake. But don't worry, everything is going to be fine." He stated as he climbed out of the bed. "I'm going to take a shower now, I have to be at the airport in two hours." Faith nodded her head in reply, but still couldn't shake the uneasy feeling she was having.

As the morning sun rose off the waters of the beach. Sin sat on the hood of the car, and took in the beauties of life. His mind was filled with images from distant past, as he contemplated what had to be done. By now his plan was now in motion, and there was no stopping it. In just a few hours fate's will be sealed, but who's? Only time will tell.

"Are you B.B?" "And you are?" "I'm Celestial, Sin sent me." "Well come in, we have a lot of work to do." B.B and Celestial began working all through the night. There was much for him to do for Celestial, and perfection was everything. His role in it all was far from small, and if not done right it would ruin everything. Once the transformation of his special effects were complete, the two set out early that morning to get into arrival. The news camera's had picked up brief moments of Murphy as he continued to observe the crowd. as the plane pulled up the door opened allowing the stairs to touch the edge pf the carpet. First to exit were two large men from the Pope's personal security team. They scanned the crowd then walked to the bottom of the steps as Jinsu entered the door way. He took a glance around as well, before waving the Pope to come on. Langley was also watching the coverage, as he sat in the safety of the White House. As Jinsu descended the steps, Lucifer stepped off the plane then stopped, and waved to the crowd. As he walked down the stairs, he whispered into Jinsu's ear. "If he was going to take a shot, he's missed his best one."

As the scope locked on it's target, the motor cage began to pull up at the end of the carpet. Murphy walked along side the Pope as they opened the bullet proof glass carriage. "POW!" The loud echo of the rifle soared through the air as the security team huddled around the Pope ushering him to his carriage. As they reached the steps of the convoy a barrage of gunshots dismantled the huddle as Celestial stepped out of the crowd firing the MK5. Murphy spun around drawing his gun. "Pow! Pow! Pow! Pow!" Four shots went into Celestial chest knocking him to the ground. Lucifer smiled as they loaded him into the convoy and locked the glass door. Murphy remained over Celestial with his gun drawn ordering the security team to get the Pope out of here. As the convoy pulled off, Jinsu approached Celestial's body as he gasped for air. He knelt down and snatched the silicone mask from his head to reveal his face. "Celestial?" He looked to the crowd then the convoy and asked. "Where is Sin!?" With his last breath Celestial smiled in Jinsu's face, before he drew his gun, then shot Celestial in the head. "BOOM!" The sudden explosion spun Murphy and Jinsu around as the back of the convoy erupted from inside. The crowd erupted in screams as Jinsu ran to the convoy. The Pope's charred body remained inside as Jinsu checked the cab looking for the release to the door. But what he found inside was a dead secret service agent and a missing driver. As the rest of the security team made it to the convoy, Jinsu began to give out orders. "Confiscate all camera's, and get those reporters out of here. Don't let them see the body, we have to get him to the Leviathan. And get that traders body to."

It was time to put my final piece of the plan together. I knew the only time the gate's of Hell would be open, was to receive the Leviathan. And that had to be on direct orders from Lucifer himself. So if phase one was complete, they would be on there way here now, and I needed to be ready to commence with phase two. "Let's go Jason." I stated pulling him from the trunk. The Leviathan was docked down on Miami harbor. I assumed phase one was a success, by the looks on the security around the ship. They were waiting for something, and I had to get on before it got here. ring.. Ring.. "Go ahead." "It's B.B you better get moving, it's done." "Good work." I tossed the phone into the water then aimed the car in the direction of the Leviathan. After doing so I placed Jason behind the wheel as I set the car in neutral. Giving it a little push, the car began to slowly roll down the pier. I walked a long the secondary pier as the guards attention became focused on Jason and the car. The closer he got the more alarmed they became. One of the guards stepped out holding up his hand to halt the vehicle as he yelled out commands. "That's far enough. This is a private area, turn back now, or we will open fire." As the car continued to roll closer, the guards brandished their gun's as panic set in. "I said halt!" Bop! Bop! Bop! Bop! As the crew began to open fire. I lowered myself into the water and swam over to the ship. As they continued to fire more assistance real down from the ship. Bullets ripped through Jason's body covering the car in holes as the men continued to shoot until the car came to a stop. As the deck cleared I climbed out of the water and crept aboard the Leviathan while they focused on inspecting the carnage. I was sure Jason's appearance was one of unrecognizable detail by now. But what did I care, phase two was complete. Now all I had to do was find a place to hide and wait.

"Murphy! You're new to the team, and you don't know me, but get to fast. When I tell you to move you move, and if I give you an order I expect it to be done. Now get on the phone with air traffic control, and alert them of our arrival. Then get Langley on the phone, and have him arrange for a helicopter to be waiting when we land." "Yes Sir, but if I may ask, who shall I say the order is coming from?" "Tell them Jinsu, is the one in control now."

"Do,na, na, Do, na, na." "Today in Braking news, for those of us that have been following the coverage of the Pope's arrival here today, got a shocking turn of events occurred here moments ago. From what we're being told, this was a failed attempt of an assassination on our beloved Pope. Witnesses say it was a horrible scene as the convoy erupted in a fire explosion. We have not yet spoken with or seen the Pope to confirm these allegations. But we pray for the best, and hope that you will stay with us as we continue to cover this story and more shocking developments.

Jinsu turned the T.V off and leaned back in his seat as he replayed the events in his mind. On one hand he congratulated Sin for a game well played. Sin was proving to be more than they had given him credit for. But on the other hand, he couldn't help but wonder, where Sin was, and what he would do next. For sure he thought he would come for him next, but seeing as he wasn't a public figure. Jinsu wouldn't make it easy to be found. "Sir, Langley's on the phone." Murphy stated handing Jinsu the phone. "Go ahead Langley." "Jinsu what the hell happened?" "Not now Langley, I'm sure you seen exactly what happened. And I'd appreciate it if you don't talk to me like I'm one of your subordinates." "My mistake Jinsu, forgive me." "What is the status of that helicopter?" "The chopper is ready, there was one already on standby." "Alert the Leviathan, tell them I'll be there in thirty minutes. And have them ready to leave." "Will do Sir."

Langley hung up the phone and immediately contacted the captain of the Leviathan. "Captain inform your men that the Leviathan is set to depart in thirty minutes." "Yes Sir, but on who's authority?" "Jinsu's."

The captain hung up the phone then pressed the emergency departure alarm. As the red lights flashed through the ship, Sin drew Destruction thinking he had been discovered as he hid in the storage unit. The captain grabbed the microphone and began to speak over the intercom. "All crew report to your stations and prepare for immediate departure." This gave Sin a sigh of relief as he ducked into the shadow's. The captain then grabbed his radio and called to his security team. "Sergeant come in." "Go ahead captain." "What has come of that situation out there?" "It's been taken care of. Just some drunk going the wrong way." "Well clean it up, and get back to the ship. Our guess should be arriving." "Will do Sir." The sergeant got off the radio and began to instruct his men. "Listen up, we need to move this car. You three roll this piece of shit into the water. The rest of you on me, return to the ship and prepare to leave." The commando's followed their sergeant back to the ship as the other three disposed off the vehicle and await the arrival of their guest.

As the plane landed on the tarmac Jinsu waisted no time as the door to the plane opened. He stood in the door way observing the area as the plane slowed to a stop near the helicopter. "Let's move!" He yelled as he exited the plane and boarded the chopper. Murphy came out second as he helped to carry Celestials body. "Get those body's loaded and find a seat." Murphy climbed inside and strapped himself in as the helicopter took off. "Where we headed Sir?" "To the Harbor." Jinsu replied to the pilot. As the helicopter crossed over the city. Murphy couldn't help but think of Faith, and how just some time ago, he was tracking Sin through this very city. "Alright. Phone off. I don't need anyone giving off our location." Jinsu yelled as they drew closer to the harbor. As they began to land, Jinsu stepped out first, always taking lead. Murphy and the two other guards carried the body's off as they made their way to the ship. "Excuse me Sir, this is a private area." One of the ships guards stated as Jinsu approached. "Step aside; I think you'll find that we're being expected." The three guards clutched their weapons in response to Jinsu's demeanor. "We're on orders to check all identification before letting anyone through." "I understand; Ray." He called to the large man carrying the Pope's corpse over his shoulder. As the man drew his gun Jinsu reacted thrusting his fist inside the guards chest, then flung his life less body to the side. He grabbed the second guard by the neck breaking it. "Pow!" A single shot went into the third guards head as his attention focused on Jinsu. "Good working Ray." "Anytime." "Man that felt good." Gins replied shaking the blood from his hand as they proceeded to the ship. There was no need for Jinsu to kill the guards, he merely just wanted to flex his power. And that he did, as Murphy now understood why he was calling the shots. "Take the body's to the lower deck, and put them in the storage unit." Jinsu ordered as he and the captain retired to the control room. "Lead the way big Ray." Murphy stated having this being his first time on the ship. "Follow me." "Long time Jinsu." "Captain." "So where are we headed?" "To the triangle, we're going through the gates." "Alright men you heard him, let's set a course for Bermuda. It's time we take the ship home."

As they reached the storage room, Ray laid the Pope's body on the floor, while the other man flung his end of Celestial's body in the corner. "Damn! You couldn't at least tell me you were going to throw the body." Murphy complained still holding onto Celestial's feet. "Just tuck the trader in over there, and let's get back upstairs." The man replied as they walked out of the door.

Ding.. Ding. Murphy looked up hearing the tapping of metal as he knelt beside Celestial's body. He knew the sound had come from the shadow's, but he couldn't see anything. When a hand suddenly appeared grabbing Murphy by the mouth. His eye's widened as Sin's face emerged. He lifted a finger to his lips to keep Murphy from shouting as he released him. "Man what the hell are you doing here?" He whispered as Sin knelt down placing his hand on Celestial's chest. "Murphy, go close the door." As Murphy secured the door he watched as Sin's arm's began to glow. Before long Murphy watched as the light transferred over to Celestial's body. As it did, the four wounds in his chest began to heal. Sin placed his hand over Celestial's mouth at the same moment his eye's opened. "Shhh.

Don't speak to loud we're on the Leviathan." "Looks like it all worked out." "Yeah; and your grace is back where it belongs. I think you're going to need it where we're going." "I agree; that was a hell of an idea to use the computer system on the sniper rifle as a decoy." "They had to believe I was there to. There was no way we both would been able to sneak on board." "Man, will somebody please tell me what is going on, what are you talking about?" Murphy interrupted. "Murphy, do you know where we are going?" "No; I don't know anything, will someone inform me for a change." "We're going into the gates of Hell."

Chapter 15

" **A**lright listen up, because we don't have long before their wondering where you are. So here's the plan; Once the ship has crossed over, Murphy you'll take lead. There going to want you to bring the body's to Lucifer. As you get to the inner sanctuary I'll then create a diversion allowing you and Celestial to roam free." "Free to do what?" "Celestial knows what he is to do; find your family. As for you Murphy =, I think you should take this opportunity to find, and retrieve your soul." "How do I do that?" "Any soul of personnel interest to Lucifer won't be kept with the rest of them. They'll be in the inner chambers." "I got it, and what about you?" "Don't worry about me, that angel Seraph doesn't want this angel soul stuck down there as much as I don't want to be, that's my insurance policy." "Sin do not mistake thinking you know the mind of Seraph. He is just as likely to write her soul off as another fallen." "Celestial's right Sin, that's a big gamble." "Yeah; but if calvary doesn't come for me, there will be no more faith or hope in the world, and I don't think he wants to risk that." "Well lets hope for the best then." "Agreed; Celestial I think you're going to need this." Sin replied handing over destruction to him. "If things get too crazy you get out of there, both of you." "I understand." "Once we have the souls how do we get out of there?" Murphy asked. "I still have friends in these low places. We just have to get back to the ship. I'm sure by then, all the attention will be focused on Sin." "Then it's settled." "Not yet, what about Faith? If you don't make it, what happens to her?" "Nothing; Faith will continue to live a normal life, but when she dies she will remain in me, wherever I am." "Let's hope it doesn't come to that." "Lets; but now you have to get upstairs." Murphy turned away then exited the room. He didn't know what Sin really had planned for his end game. But he wasn't going in unprepared, letting him risk Faith. Before heading up stairs, Murphy decided he'll step into the armory as he passed the door.

"What is it Celestial? You seem troubled." "Sin I didn't want to say anything in front of Murphy, but we both know you don't have the power to take on Hell alone. And now that you've given me my grace back, you're even less stronger then you were." "Don't worry Celestial, like I said, the angels will never let one of there own suffer here. Besides this soul feed's off the faith and hope of the people, so I need you to believe. As long as we do, I'll grow stronger." "There is no faith or hope Sin, and the only weapon we have that can kill the Jins while in Hell is destruction, and I don't think that's enough." "I don't need to kill them Celestial, just keep them at bay. This ship has an armory, the weapons in it can kill demons, as for the Jin, I just need to hold them off." "If you say so Sin. But listen, if you find yourself in a bind there are inly three things that can end them while in these realms. That's Celestial's beings, that means us physically, and weapons made from either Heaven or Hell." "I'll remember that." "You do so."

"Captain how long?" "We're approaching the triangle now." As the ship continued to sail across the ocean, it finally reached the triangles point of no return. And in the blink of an eye, it vanished. The waters of the ocean now became a sea of fire. The ship appeared as if it was floating on lave or being carried by the out stretched arms of burning souls reaching for help. As Murphy felt the sudden change in the atmosphere, loaded two Mac tens, grabbing a smoke grenade, and one frag grenade then headed for the storage room. As he exited the armory, he could hear Jinsu's voice, followed by a few pair of foot steps coming down the stairs. "Murphy!" He called as Murphy walked down the hall. "Yeah." "Where have you been?" "The truth; right here. I couldn't find my way around here." "It's understandable, help them get the body's upstairs." "Yes Sir." As the three men made there way to the storage room, Murphy made it a point to announce their arrival by speaking out loud in an attempt to alert Sin. "I guess it's showtime then." Big Ray stopped and looked at Murphy for a moment then opened the door. Murphy reached under his shirt and griped the handle of one of the guns not knowing what was going to be on the other side. As they walked in they found the room in the same condition as it was when they left. "One of you grab the Pope, and I'll grab this one." "You sure about that Ray? I mean, we can handle that one." "Just do as I tell you." "No problem." Murphy replied picking up the burnt corpse. The men carried the body's to the top deck, where they met up with Jinsu. Murphy stood in amazement as he reached the top deck. He watched as men with burned wings flow from cliff to cliff watching their every move. "Murphy; throw that body into the lake." Gins ordered. As he did Murphy suddenly felt Jinsu's hand grab his shoulder. As he looked back he noticed a pair of damaged wings extending from his back. In one massive leap Jinsu took flight, carrying Murphy with him. "Ray; don't react." Celestial whispered into his ear as hung over Ray's shoulder. "I'm here for my family, where are they?" "How are you still alive Celestial?" "How are any of us?"

Ray and Celestial had been long term friends since the beginning of creation. He was the sole instrument that saved Celestial that tragic day on the Mary Celeste. And has been the very same one keeping him hidden, as he informed him on every move set against him. "Celestial, your family is here, but.." "But what?" "Celestial; no mortal flesh can survive here, unless it is that of a demon, an angel, or a Jin." "What are you saying Ray?" "Your family remains here, but only as souls." A heart breaking pain came over Celestial, as tears built up in his eyes. He knew they wouldn't survive, but the reality of the pain they must have suffered had finally set in. "You have to take me to them Ray." "Even if I did, how are you planning to get out?" "With your help."

Sin began to make his way off the ship as the sounds of silence seemed to cover the halls. All the crew from the lower level had already done. Where to he could only imagine. With the ship being docked safely behind the gates, there was no need for anyone to guard it. Sin would have to move fast, if he was going to help Murphy and Celestial. Too much time had already gone by, and he had no idea where they were.

As I made my way into the armory, I thought it was best to stock up on artillery. I grabbed the strap of an automatic shotgun and hung it across my back. I then tucked two side arm pistols into my waist band, then grabbed an M16. "Click." "Don't move; who are you? And what are you doing on this ship?" The sergeant asked pressing his gun to the back of my head. "Listen, I was.. Um." "Pow!" I ducked my head and spun around, striking him in the ribs with the butt of the rifle, as his gun went off barely missing me.

"What was that?" "What was what?" "Did you not just hear a gun shot? Put me down, and get back to the ship. Wait for me there, when you see me coming cover me." Celestial ordered. "Don't be long Celestial." "I'm right behind you." Ray ran back to the ship as Celestial continued to the dungeon. Jinsu had taken Murphy high up into the tower of Lucifer's Castle. He couldn't understand what he could possibly want from him, as he clutched the handles of the two guns under his shirt, and waited as he stared out of a window. Hell appeared to him as any other place would, only covered in flames, and red stone with a lake of molting lava. It was like a city inside of a volcano. "Jinsu, why are we here?" "We're here for your protection." "Protection from what?" "Sin." "He's here?" "I'm sure of it. Why he wants to be here, I don't know. But since he does, I allowed him. Now we must make sure he doesn't leave." "But how do you know he's here?" "When we were on the peer, I noticed the tail light of a car sticking out of the water. When I asked the Captain about it, he said it was just an incident with some drunk. The likely hood of that is none. I knew then something was up. And who else would have interest in this ship?" "Is that why all these people are running to the ship?" Jinsu walked over to the window and became furious from what he saw. Murphy pulled the pins from both grenades, then backed away from the window. He counted seven seconds then rolled the grenades at Jinsu's feet, as he continued to stare out of the window. "BOOM!"

As I continued to wrestle with the commando, time was slipping away from one. I Had to do something fast, and now, "POW!" As we wrestled over the M16, a single gun shot went off. I stood stunned as the sergeants head opened up. I took control of the gun and pointed it at the man standing in the doorway. "You're with Celestial right?" "And you're Ray." "Welcome back Annunaki." "Let's hope it's not for long." Ray and I began to make our way to the top deck. "Ray, get to the control room, and start the ship." As he did I ran out onto the outer deck firing the M16 at the crew members trying to board the ship.

"Damn it; I guess it started already." Celestial thought to himself as a loud explosion caused the ground to shake underneath his feet. As he continued through the dungeon, he found no traces of his family. The sudden sound of running feet caused him to hide as guards ran pass taking a stairway up into the castle. As he hid Celestial noticed a black door, at the end of a corridor, and decided to inspect it. Once he got to the door, he pulled the handle only to find that it was locked. Celestial raised destruction and in one loud roar, he had blown a hole in whee the lock once was. As the light from the hall crept into the room, Celestial's eye's where met with Sin's shackled soul.

The explosion in the tower had knocked Jinsu out of the window. Murphy then drew his guns, running out of the room as the smoke filled. Jinsu extended his wings breaking his fall as he flew back to the hole that was now in the side of the castle. He attempted to see through the smoke as he hovered around the hole. But the smoke had now completely filled the room.

As they attempted to over run the ship, I found myself running low on ammunition. The M16 had completely run out, and the shot gun was soon to be next. I watched as the Jin's circled above me like vultures, periodically swooping down at me. I needed to draw them away from the ship. "BOOM!" A large explosion erupted from the tower of the castle. This was just what I needed. As the Jin's began to fly back to the castle, I dropped the shotgun drawing two pistols and ran for the edge of the ship. As I dodged, under punches, kicking people into the lake. I drove off the edge of the ship.

Murphy ran through the halls searching every room. When he stopped as he ran into a room with a woman inside. "Who are you?" The woman cried as Murphy pointed the gun at her. "The devil, now tell me where they keep the souls." "There all around you." "This ain't no time to be funny bitch." "It's Mary, not bitch." Instantly Murphy had remembered the name Mary, from Sin's and Celestial's conversation. "Is your name Celeste?" "How did you know that?" "Someone's here looking for you." "Who?" I'll explain later, but right now you have to come with me." "I'm not going anywhere with you, and you'll explain now." "Pow! Pow!" "Ahh!" Mary screamed as Murphy shot her twice in the leg. "what is wrong with you?" She yell'ed as he hurled her over his shoulder. "Wait." Murphy spun around and pointed his gun at a man who was shackled to a wall. "Please don't shoot." "What do you want?" "I can help you get what you're searching. But you have to help me get out of here." "And who are you?" "My name is Enki." "I can't carry you both, so just tell me where the souls are." "Even if I did, once you've regained your soul you wont be able to survive in hell. But I can help you, I can give you strength." "How?" "Take my hand." Murphy hesitated as he thought for a moment. Indeed he couldn't trust this man, this had all seemed to strange. But what other choice did he have. He didn't want to stay in hell, and if he left his soul, he would always be bound to it's will. He knelt down and dropped the gun as he took Enki's hand. "Ahhh!" He yell'ed as his arm began to glow, and catch a flame. And in the very next instant, Enki the winged serpent was gone.

"Jinsu; are you alright?" One of the Jin asked as they surrounded him. "Yes; I'm fine. Get back to the ship, and don't let him leave here." Jinsu ordered as he watched Sin run through the streets of hell. I had suddenly led the crew away from the ship as they chased me into an old burning building. I didn't know how long I could keep this up. I was low on ammunition, and close to being corned. And there was still no sign of Murphy and Celestial.

Murphy lifted the gun then rose to his feet, as he could instantly feel the change in him. He could no longer even feel the weight of the woman he carried. As he began to leave images of the dungeon played inside his mind. He knew then that was where he needed to be heading, to find his soul. "Murphy!" Celestial yell'ed as he came up the dungeon stairwell. "Where dod you come from?" "The tower, you?" "The dungeon." "did you find what you were looking for?" "No; but I dud find something for you." Celestial raised his hand placing it on Murphy's chest, as he restored his soul. As he did Celestial's face became one of confusion as Murphy's eye's began to change two different colors. "Here, look what I found for you." Murphy replied placing Mary on her feet. "Mary; but how?"" "After all this time Celestial, you finally returned for me." "But how are you alive Mary? What have you done?" "I did what anyone would have done to survive. I had to stop the pain." "Where is my daughter/" "She's not here. Her fate was not like mine. Having being half human, and half Jin, Lucifer raised her to be apart of his army." "Where is she!" "I'm sorry to cut this short, but we need to go." "Murphy's right, we need to get out of here."

I ran upstairs and locked myself in a room as I barricaded the door and prepared for my final stand. So I thought, before the roof began collapsing down as Jinsu came crashing through into the room. "No more games Annunaki." He said as he rose from his knee, drawing a sword from his back. "I agree; no more games then." I lifted one of the guns and began firing at whims we charged towards each other. I ducked under the blade as he swung his sword trying to decapitate me. Jinsu was very skilled I must admit. As I blocked the sword with the guns, firing back as I continued to try and shoot him. He managed to dodge my counters with one of his own. For every slash he took I returned a gun shot. We were back and forward on the attack. I would swing the gun at his head, and he would dodge, countering with a strike of his own. Many time's we were able to land a blow as we kicked and punched each other, but never letting the weapons land. "Click, Click." As the gun's ran empty Jinsu Locked on my left arm slinging me against a wall. His blade followed intended for my neck. I immediately jammed the barrel of both gun's under my chin, blocking the blade. As Jin's continued to press the blade against the gun's, the wall gave out behind me. We fell through the wall into the hallway on top of a burning pile of rubble. The demons waiting on the other side, watched as Jinsu continued to try and press the blade through the guns. "It's over Sin, this is and angel blade. Stronger then the metal of your gun's. Just look at them, the damage they took just from you countering. It wont be long, and when you're dead, I'm going to take every last one go your souls." He was right, the gun's were on the verge of collapsing. So I did the only thing I could do. "Hoooc, Thoooo." I spit a hard loogie into Jinsu's eyes, enraging him as he pulled the blade away, and began pounding me with his bare fist. I reached for a piece of burning rubble with my left hand, and swung it at his head. Jinsu caught my arm slamming it back to the ground, and continued to pound me with his other hand. "Plat! Plat! Plat! Plat! Plat!" A barrage of gunfire sounded outside the building causing Jinsu to look up. I reached with my right hand for another piece of rubble, this time landing the blow. as Jinsu dismounted me, I rolled to my feet and attempted to run for the window. I staggered and swung widely as I pressed through the mob of demons filling the hall. They continued to punch and kick me, preventing me from going any further. When suddenly Jinsu got to his feet and came charging at me. "Ahhhh!" He yelled grabbing the top of my head, then running it through a wall. He followed pulling my head back through as he slung me against the opposite wall.Then continued with a huge elbow strike across my temple and a devastating blow to my

"What are you doing?" One of the demons asked. "He said to watch him. What better way then this? I'd hate to be the one that let him get away." While Mary kept them distracted with her words, she placed her hand on Sin's chest and began to restore his soul. "What's going on? What the hell are you doing? Shoot him." The man yelled as Sin's body lit up. As the man began to approach, Sin's eye's opened burning with flames. He snatched destruction from Mary's hand and jumped to his feet. "What are you going to do with only one gun?" The man asked as the demons closed in. I grabbed Mary and carried her on my back. Then suddenly the first mortar shell dropped. "BOOM!" Murphy and Ray began to open fire with the 50 calibers keeping the Jin at bay. Celestial then started the mortar shelling on my location, as he fired up the aircraft destroyer machine guns to aid Murphy and Ray. The ship had already started moving, and I had a long way to run. As the first shell blew a hole in the crowd, I took off running carrying Mary on my back. Celestial kept the shelling close to my position to keep the demons off of me. I jumped from stone to stone as the explosions disturbed the ground, causing it to separate as molten hot magma shot up. I wasn't going to make it, we weren't moving fast enough. "BOOM!" "Ahh." The shock wave from Jinsu slamming into the ground knocked me over, causing Mary to go flying as I rolled on the ground. "Did you think, I was going to really let you leave Annunaki?" "Mary; keep going." Mary did as I asked and got to her feet as she continued running for the ship. "You know she'll never make it, the ship is too far, and my Jin will stop her before then. Shall we finish this?" "Let's." I drew destruction and waited as eh charged towards me. Then opened fire on the ground, causing it to crumble beneath him. As Jinsu fell through the ground, I took off running firing at the Jin that swooped down towards Mary. As I cleared a path she continued to run until she came to the edge of a cliff. There was no way she could reach the ship. I glanced back as Jinsu emerged from the ground with lava spurting up behind him. Sin's body began to light up as he ran harder and faster. Gins dove in chasing slightest idea of what you've done? This little debacle of yours has released the seal of the horse men of war. You broke the covenant, no angel of God is to pass through the gate's of Hell. And now because of you that gate is broken. Every creature and being of Hell will be released. You've brought war upon us, so no; you want be returning to Hell. But you wont stay here either." Seraph then took his slamming sword and ran it through Sin's chest. As the blade passed through him, Sin looked over to the door of the lower deck as he noticed Aknubious smiling as he closed the door. And in a blink of an eye, Seraph and Sin were gone.

Epilogue

The Best of Purgatory

As Celestial awoke, he found Ray standing over him. "Where is Sin?" He asked as he surveyed the deck. "Help me up." "Take it easy Celestial. He's not here anymore, Sin's gone." "What do you mean? Murphy!" Celestial called out as Murphy stood at the edge of the deck, over looking the water. "Murphy!" He called again, but still he was unresponsive. Murphy then looked over his shoulder with a cold stare like death and replied. "My name is Enki, address me as so." And in one massive leap, wings spread from his back, and he was gone.

As all the Heavenly host gathered together in the throne room of God, Lucifer stood trial. "And what do you have to say for yourself now? You who wanted to reign Sun God. I gave you your own domain, and look at what you've done with it. Now Enki has run free, and the horse men of war has mounted his horse and set out to do his work. Nations will come against nations all in the name of their new deity's. Is this what you wanted? Don't speak! Now that Annunaki is gone there is no more faith and hope in the world. There will only be war." "And what about Enki? What will he do?" The council of heavenly host asked. "Enki will try to open Purgatory and release the other deity's to increase his power and army." "And what will you do?" Lucifer asked as he spoke up. "Enough from you, depart from me morning star. We are finished here."

As Sin laid unconscious on the shores of the beach. he awoke as the waves continued to splash on his face. He rolled onto his side grabbing his chest where Seraph's sword once was. "You're finally awake." A voice said as he looked up. "Who are you?" "I'm six, you're lucky I found you. I've been here watching over you." "For what?" "Predators; Everything here is looking to eat each other, and take your power." "And where is here?" "Purgatory." Six replied as Sin rose to his feet in amazement, of the great jungle labyrinth.